# OUTRAGE:
# HITLER DIDN'T DIE

# Outrage:
## Hitler Didn't Die

Joel M. Reed

**PB**

POLUS BOOKS
NEW YORK

# Outrage: Hitler Didn't Die

Copyright © 2013 - 2020 by Joel M. Reed

Polus Books
New York

ISBN: 978-1-942183-12-9

## Prologue

Simon Blake was commanding the lead tank in the column, high balling into Steinhoffen with indifference, because his unit was assured by Intelligence that there would be no opposition. Suddenly, automatic weapons fire began to play against the armor plate of the Sherman, and a Panzerfurst round hit the M-4's right hand tread and knocked it off. The tank skid awkwardly and another rocket smashed into its engine compartment. Simon ordered his crew to bail out and then leaped from the turret, scrambling to the relative safety of a church wall while the units to his rear covered him with fire.

As he lay flat in a puddle of icy water with chips of masonry raining down the back of his neck he unholstered his .45 automatic, cocked it, and shot ineffectually in the general direction of the enemy until his driver grabbed him by the ankles and pulled him around a corner just before the Sherman exploded. Simon, who loved that particular tank more than any person in his life, cursed the Germans silently and then checked to see if all of his crew had made it to safety before crawling back to Ray Warren's tank which was zeroing in on the Stadt house with tracers from its .50 caliber machine gun. Simon picked up the outside phone and shouted to Ray, "You got room for me?"

The unshaven lieutenant replied in a calm, Midwestern drawl, "Fall back, knuckle head."

Simon stuck the phone back into its box and led his crew carefully away from the fire fight. His company commander, Captain Morris Ankhorn, a stocky, red faced attorney of Pennsylvania Dutch descent, was conferring with an infantry company commander two blocks to the rear of the action. Simon walked up to him and said, "I need a new tank."

"Relax," said Ankhorn.

"*Relax?*"

"Relax, youngster! The war will be over before you get a new tank."

"Crap!"

"Take a break!" growled Ankhorn. "I've got to see what's holding us up here."

Having nothing better to do, Simon crossed over to a medic who was working on a young rifleman with a leg wound. He knelt down by the boy, offered him a smoke, and asked, "How are you doing, kid?"

The casualty smiled and said, "Some shit, isn't it? The war is almost over. What? A couple of more hours? A day?"

"Yeah, some shit!" said Simon. His eyes fell on a bandoleer of ammunition that the medic had removed from the wounded kid. Simon stood up, retrieved it, and without a word, a stretcher bearer handed him the downed boy's M-1 rifle. Simon ejected the half spent clip it contained, reloaded it, and adjusted the elevation and windage to suit his eye. Crossing the street, he again imposed himself on Ankhorn, looking for orders.

The captain said, "The Burgermeister says there's some SS in the Stadt house."

"Screw the Burgermeister! Let's pull back and bomb the shit out of this place."

"No, I got a squad pinned down across the street from the Stadt house," said the infantry officer wondering why he always had to explain himself to Simon, an enlisted man.

The sound of a honking horn intruded on the gunfire reverberating off the walls on either side of the narrow street. A brand new, spanking clean jeep followed by a 2 ½ -ton truck towing a radio trailer squeezed between a tank destroyer and an idle 60 millimeter mortar crew and stopped. Simon had to smile at the sight of the new arrivals. They all wore neatly tailored uniforms, ties, and shiny brass. A Second Lieutenant who wasn't far out of his teens leaped off the jeep and strode over to Ankhorn, saluted sharply, and then demanded, "Would you tell me what the hell is going on here, Sir?"

Ankhorn's jaw dropped. "Tell you what? We have a bit of a fire fight on our hands."

"Bullshit!" replied the neatly tailored Lieutenant. "There's no resistance in Steinhoffen!"

A comic opera played across Ankhorn's face. He said, deliciously, "I take it you guys are with some sort of intelligence unit?"

The Lieutenant snapped, "The OSS and you got it all fucked up! There's no resistance here!"

Ankhorn stuck his nose right into the young officer's face and spat, "Sonny, you tell that to the Krauts holed up in the Stadt house."

"Thank you, I think I will," said the Lieutenant. He saluted, did a perfect about face, and re-mounted the jeep. As every G.I. in the area looked on in amazement, the jeep and the truck behind it started up and headed directly towards the Stadt house. Ankhorn shouted after them, "You assholes! The whole street is under fire."

Ignoring Ankhorn, the two vehicles continued around the corner to receive the attention of almost every weapon in the Stadt house. The Jeep braked to a halt, backed up, and made one of the fastest U-turns in history, skidding back around the corner and sideswiping the truck pulling the trailer. Simon, Ankhorn, the infantry officer, and a couple of medics ran up to the jeep.

"Are you guys all right?" asked Ankhorn.

The Lieutenant caught his breath, bit his lip, and then said, "We're going to wait back by the bridge. Please notify me as soon as Steinhoffen is secure."

"We sure will," said Ankhorn with satisfaction. The jeep backed up to disengage itself from the truck and then sped off in the direction it had come. Ankhorn looked at Simon and winked.

Simon said, "I'll be sure to remind you to notify them, Captain."

"You do that," said Ankhorn. "Now how about hauling ass back to the rear and finding our mess sergeant and see if he can get a hot meal up to us when we secure this shit hole." Ankhorn looked down at his watch and then said, "There's no way we're going to push past this town before dark."

Simon turned to his crew, who were dogging at his heel, and said, "Did you hear that? Hustle up some hot chow." Pointing to his driver he said, "And see about getting us a fresh tank."

His gunner asked, "What about you, Sarge?"

"I'm going to see about billets for the night and a little loot. I just had two Liecas burn up on me."

Simon started off towards the corner at a crouch. Ankhorn ran up to him and caught him by his collar.

"Where the hell do you think you're going? Isn't it a little too late in the war to play soldier?"

"Shit, Captain," replied Simon. "I'm a big city boy, not a hero. I'm going to find you a decent C.P."

"Simon!"

"Loot! If I don't move fast the infantry will clear this place out before us."

Simon ran to the corner where he flung himself flat against the ground and crawled forward to get a look down the street on which his tank had been hit. The Americans were throwing everything they had at the Stadt house, but no one was moving forward. The war was too close to an end to take risks. Simon rose to a crouch, dashed around the corner and into a shallow doorway and from there began to sidle against the blown out shop windows toward a house on the next block. He thought he'd seen a brass plate on it just before his tank was hit. A brass plate meant doctor, and he figured that if this was a doctor's house there would be valuables in it and the possibility of a bath tub and the even more remote possibility of hot water.

He half-crawled, half-ran, followed by a squad of infantry, who had been trying to lob rifle grenades into the windows of the Stadt house from doorways along the street, and a heavy weapons squad with a recoilless rifle. As they pressed forward, an A.P. round smashed into the facade of the Stadt house sending a grotesque gargoyle crashing to the ground.

As Simon glared back at it, he heard chimes and looked up to discover that the A.P. round had activated the mechanism of the Stadt house's glockenspiel. A chubby, red faced, dancing baker carrying a tray appeared in the tower. The G.I.'s cheered and then turned their fire onto the ornate figure and blew it to bits.

The door of the house with the brass plaque was locked. An unshaven, hooked nose infantry corporal of Armenian descent said, "Kick it in!"

Simon stepped out into the street to aim at the lock and felt two bullets cut the air near his head. The shots came from inside. He hit the ground and crawled back to the wall of the house and fired from a prone position up into the door, blowing the lock apart. The little Corporal kicked the door in and then rolled a grenade into the front room. After it exploded, Simon rushed inside, firing blindly from the hip, and then halted to slap another clip into the M-1. The rest of the Corporal's squad rushed past him, clearing each room of the house with a grenade before entering it.

Simon leaped into a small parlor on his right. A portrait of Hitler hung over a coal fireplace. He smashed his rifle butt into it over and over again with such force that he drove most of the picture and the glass covering it into the plaster behind.

When he kicked open the door to a small treatment room, Simon thought that he had just captured a top secret, German weapon. It was a moment before he realized that he was staring at a primitive X-ray machine. He went through a couple of drawers, studied a wooden stethoscope he found on a table, and, as he was leaving, spotted a glint on the floor. He bent down and found an ancient brass microscope under a pile of plaster gauged out of the wall by a shell. Simon studied it for a moment, noticed that the mirror was cracked, and tossed it aside.

He then took the steps two at a time to the second floor toilet which was equipped with a cramped, tin tub. It wasn't what he was looking for.

The infantry had gotten up to the floor above to fire down into the Stadt house, the recoilless rifle making an awful woosh as it shot shell after shell at the same target from a bad angle. Simon slid into a bedroom facing the Stadt house and tried to get a view of the fire fight in progress without exposing himself, wondering when the Germans would wise up and surrender.

Through one of the Stadt house's first floor windows he saw a blur crawling across the floor. He raised the M-1, aimed, and fired an entire clip. Whatever it was stopped moving.

The little Corporal came running down the steps and looked in the door. "Are you okay?"

"I got one," said Simon.

The Corporal sidled over to Simon and said, "That damn place is built like a fort. Next step is either the Air Corps or some idiot rushing over there and dumping grenades in the windows."

"Don't look at me!" said Simon. "I just came along to grab a good billet for tonight."

"I just thought since you're always playing cowboys and Indians—"

"In a tank, asshole," said Simon. "What's behind the Stadt house?"

"How should I know? I hope the rest of our column by now."

Simon ran to a room at the rear of the house and looked out another window. The corporal asked, "What are you thinking about?"

"A hot bath," replied Simon. He then said, "You probably could outflank them. There's no windows on this side of the Stadt house. If you circle behind the building and make a lot of noise, they may surrender."

"They're SS"

"They'll still fucking surrender."

"We'll cover you," said the Corporal.

"Bull," said Simon. He turned and ran down the steps and out the back door of the house and then into a little garden. The fence facing the street was unmarred by fire. Simon found a door in it and opened it cautiously, shouting, "Hello!" at the same time.

Someone called back in English and Simon looked right to discover one of the tanks from his unit down at the far corner with a platoon of infantry. Simon walked casually up to it. Its commander was a Sergeant named Dorner who Simon didn't get along with. Simon shouted up at him, "What are you guys doing back here? You can move up on the flank of the building with your infantry."

Dorner shouted back, "The war's almost over, Blake."

"Okay! Get out of the turret and I'll do it for you."

"Fuck you," replied Dorner.

Simon gave him a stiff finger and, without knowing why, shouted, "Cover me!" He ran back into the doctor's house, up to the third floor, grabbed the hooked nosed Corporal and said, "I'm going in by the side."

"By yourself?"

"I want to see if I draw any fire."

"Take a couple of grenades," the Corporal called out.

Simon waited, flat on his face in the garden, until the Corporal's squad began to fire blindly into the buildings facing the right side of the Stadt house in case they housed any snipers. He then dashed across the street and took cover on the opposite side. When he realized that no one was shooting at him, he slowed his pace, crossed the intersection, and went around to the side of the Stadt house. The face of the building was still under heavy American fire. Simon tried the huge, iron braced door before him, couldn't budge it, and then ran back to Dorner's tank and motioned it forward.

The Sherman turned the corner, grinding the curb stones into dust and fired a high explosive round, completely demolishing the door. The riflemen ran forward and took positions on both sides of the entranceway. Simon joined them, peered into a vaulted passage, and then with a shrug, followed it into a circular courtyard.

The roar of the firefight outside barely penetrated the courtyard which had a heavy, dank medieval air about it. An undamaged Veeblewagon was parked to one side in front of a row of wooden shed-like buildings whose odor identified them as stables. No one, including Simon, seemed ready to go any further.

Simon heard the engine of a tank behind him and turned in amazement to discover Dorner's Sherman squeezing through the narrow arcade with less than an inch to spare on either side. Some shouted, "Krauts," and Simon turned as two SS officers in immaculate uniforms came out of the rear door of the Stadt house proper and headed towards the Veeblewagon.

Catching sight of Simon out of the corner of his eye, the first officer stopped, spun around, and brought up the submachine he carried. Simon calmly shot him from a standing position, the M-1's .30 Caliber rounds continuing the officer's spin and knocking him clear off his feet onto his back. The SS man behind stopped and froze with his hands in the air. As Simon relieved him of his Luger pistol, Dorner's tank stopped beside him.

Dorner yelled down from the turret, "The Stadt house surrendered."

Simon shouted back, "You fucking idiot, what did you expect to do with your tank in here? You got no room to swing your gun and all your shells will just bounce back in your face."

Soon after, a dozen, very young and pale SS men in soft caps were lined up in front of a church wall and being verbally abused by an unshaven Lieutenant brandishing a Thompson submachine gun. Ray turned to Simon and drawled, "I heard you tried to take the Stadt house by yourself?"

"The infantry is going to put you in for a medal," added Captain Ankhorn.

"It was the stupidest thing I've ever done in my life!"

Ankhorn pointed to the roof of a house more than a block away from where they were standing and said, "The Burgermeister says that place has a modern bathroom. It's my C.P. Haul ass over there and grab it before the infantry does."

# 1

Simon spent little time on the West side of Manhattan and shouldn't have been there at four o'clock in the morning when he found the building. He had just driven down from his home in Rockland County averaging seventy-five miles an hour all the way with a slight pain in his chest. He'd had a mild heart attack two years before. "God damn it," he said to himself. "Children. You put all that time into them and what do you get in return? Problems!" Charlene was Simon's youngest daughter, just sixteen years old. She had left the house stating that she was going over to a friend's house in the neighborhood to do her homework. She didn't return until well after two am. She casually admitted that she had lied. That she had gone to Studio 54 and then on to a party in Soho. Simon slapped her and then fled the house when his wife raised her voice to him. He got into his Cadillac Seville and drove down towards New York City just to blow off steam.

He turned off the West side highway at 86th Street and drove downtown three more blocks before making a right turn and pulling into an empty space by a hydrant. He opened the window of the car, closed his eyes, and breathed deeply.

When he opened his eyes again he saw the building for the first time. The address was 389 West 83rd Street and it occupied an odd sized plot at the corner of Riverside Drive. His trained eye told him that was erected just after the turn of the century in German Renaissance style and originally contained one apartment per floor. But, he figured, some greedy speculator got a hold of it in the Fifties and broke it up into small units. The cornerstone confused Simon. It read "1924." He thought, *Nobody built like that in 1924.*

The structure appealed to Simon. He liked older parcels of real estate with a flair. "Hell, I could have picked it up in the Sixties for twenty thousand cash."

Simon got out of his car and entered the lobby. He noted that the marble on the walls and floor had been so well fitted that you could barely see a seam and that the inner door was solid brass and the few, remaining, original glass panes were hand etched.

The remainder of the lobby was a mess. A cheap fluorescent fixture overhead and a peeling, brass-plated bell board crudely installed in one wall. When he looked through the inner door, he saw an elegant crystal chandelier hanging from the ceiling, still at least ninety-five percent intact, with a coating of dust an inch thick.

It wasn't until Simon had returned to his car and turned back for a last look at the building that he discovered there was a carving above the front door. He returned to the entrance to take a closer look. Chiseled between two, fat cherubs was the German words, *"Englischer Gartens."*

Simon was already on the George Washington Bridge headed home when another place known as the "Englischer Gartens" leapt into his mind. To say that he visited them would be much too inaccurate. He drove his new Sherman tank through them. "I saw that same, exact building before. In Munich, on Widenmayer Street on the Iser River."

Simon drove all the way back to the city, stopped off in an all-night luncheonette for coffee, and then drove back to the building to prove to himself that he wasn't fantasizing. He continued downtown to his office and went directly to the land book and made a note of the owner, the "389 West 83rd Street Corporation" in care of the law firm of Cabot, Stiles, Rothschild, and Binney.

# 2

When Terrence Litewood, a young associate who had just joined the firm, arrived at the offices of Cabot, Stiles, Rothschild, and Binney at seven-thirty in the morning to catch up on some proofreading, he found Simon waiting.

Simon rose and said, "I want to talk to you. I'm Simon Blake."

"*The* Simon Blake?" asked Litewood, rather taken aback.

"Right!" said Simon. "The one in real estate."

"Terrence Litewood," said the young lawyer, extending his hand. "What can I do for you, Mr. Blake?"

"I want to buy Three Eighty Nine, West Eighty-Third Street."

"Three Eighty Nine, West Eighty-Third Street?"

"You represent the owners," Simon informed him.

"Cabot, Stiles, Rothschild, and Binney may represent the owners," Litewood said cheerfully. "I'm not sure. Would you mind waiting in the conference room? I really can't do anything until one of the partners get here." As he escorted Simon into the conference room he marveled, "Simon Blake! I just read about you in Forbes. I'm sure one of the senior partners will want to talk to you. You're one of the richest men in the country."

"On paper," said Simon.

"I'll get you some coffee," replied Litewood.

"I don't want any coffee. I just want to buy that building. Let's get on with it."

"You should have called for an appointment. I really can't help you by myself Mr. Blake."

"It's a small deal. I didn't want to waste a telephone call."

"But what can I do?" asked Litewood.

"Pull the file yourself."

"I can't."

"I know, you're just an associate. You haven't been out of Harvard Law more than six months. You're scared shitless. Pull the file."

"Excuse me," said Litewood as he turned and hurried from the conference room down a long corridor in the partner's wing of the floor hoping that somebody with some authority had arrived early. All of the offices were empty except for the large corner one which belonged to Judge J. Foster Binney. Litewood hesitated before knocking.

Parri, a handsome man in his late thirties with just a tinge of gray, opened the door and asked, "Yes?"

"May I speak to Judge Binney for a moment?"

Parri asked, "Your name please?"

Judge Binney shouted in that certain, high pitched tone that only comes with advanced age, "Tell him to come in, Parri."

Litewood braced himself and then stepped into the Judge's office. Binney took a puff on the cigar in his mouth and said, "Who the hell are you?"

"I'm a new associate, Terrence Litewood. We haven't met yet, Judge Binney."

"What do you want?"

"Simon Blake is here."

"I don't talk to clients. I don't talk to associates either, but since you're man enough to ask for help, you've got it."

"Mr. Blake would like to buy Three Eighty Nine West—"

"No!" snapped the Judge.

"No?" said Litewood.

"N ... period ... O ... period!"

"Thank you Judge Binney. I've been looking forward to meeting you. I didn't know you came in this early."

"What else can I do in the morning? I'm eighty-five years old."

"I'll tell Mr. Blake, No."

"You don't have to," said Judge Binney. "He's standing right behind you. How do you think he made his first fifty million dollars? Taking no for an answer from piss ass little kids like you?"

"Good morning, Judge," said Simon stepping around Litewood. "You hit the nail on the head."

The Judge dismissed Litewood with a wave and gestured Simon to a chair. "Nice meeting you, Simon. Do you mind if I only call you by your first name? I gave up formalities a long time ago. Don't you dare call me Foster, though. Have some respect for your elders. You'll have coffee of course."

"Sure, Judge."

"Simon this is Parri. Parri performs a valuable service for men my age. Like seeing that I get from my limousine to this office without breaking my hip."

Simon shook hands with Parri who then backed out of the room silently. The Judge said, "I'd offer you a cigar, Simon, but we're going to get into an argument. I said no and I mean no."

"That building isn't earning up to its potential."

"The owners know all that. They do not want to sell."

"Can I— "

"No! You cannot talk to them."

"Why?"

"It's none of your business. And since you're such a nice fellow, I'll tell you another thing which you'll find out on your own anyway. The title's cloudy."

"I'll pay cash."

"It doesn't matter. Don't waste your time."

"Let me talk to the owners."

"No!"

"I'll talk to them anyway," said Simon.

"Really?" said the Judge.

"You're challenging me!"

"Simon, do you know how long I've been practicing law?"

"A long time."

"Longer than any other man alive. Do you know who I've represented in the past?"

Simon nodded.

"No, you don't! The Morgans, the Rockefellers, and I mean the originals and not the guys with Seconds and Thirds after their names. I know my law. I served in almost every high court of this State. I turned down a nomination for the Supreme Court of the United States of America. So listen to me when I speak. Don't waste your time! There's only one way you can find the owners of Three Eighty Nine and that's by getting me to tell you, which I won't!"

"We'll see about that," said Simon, getting up. "I'll pass on the coffee. I got work to do. Thanks a lot, Judge."

"For what?" asked Binney.

Simon found a metered parking space in front of 2037 Broadway. Its run-down entrance was squeezed between a liquor store with a modernized front and a dry cleaner. The glass of the front door was cracked, the doorframe warped, and the lobby's last coat of paint slapped on ten years prior and barely holding its own. The foyer smelled of urine. The white plastic letters in the directory of tenants was readable only because someone had given the glass cover a swipe with a dirty rag some time in the month past.

Simon found Max Geisler's office on the second floor next to a *Tai Chi Chuan* School and a neighborhood newspaper. He rapped on the door hoping to be heard over the sounds of a television soap opera emanating from within. After a muffled reply, Simon entered a single room cluttered with neatly bound stacks of old newspapers and magazines.

Max Geisler rose and turned the sound down on the thirteen inch set on his desk as Simon said, "My name's Simon Blake."

"Max Geisler. This is some building, huh? Did you see the lobby?" said Geisler with a nod. "The owner is waiting for somebody to tear it down and put up a high rise. He wants two million dollars for a hundred feet on upper Broadway. 'I can wait,' he says. His grandchildren will have grandchildren before they offer him that kind of money." Geisler crossed to a small, wrought iron couch with plastic cushions and cleared away two stacks of neatly bound copies of *The New York Times* to make room for Simon. "Sit down, Mr. Blake. Make yourself at home. Coffee, tea, or soda?" Geisler pointed to a small, white refrigerator in the corner.

As Simon sat, he asked, "Then you know who I am?"

"Ah," said Geisler returning to the seat behind his desk. "You're interested in Three eighty nine."

"Mr. Geisler," said Simon with a theatrical cough that was almost insincere. "I don't want you to feel insecure about my interest in the building. I know that managing it is your only source of income. Or is there more to it than that?"

"I have some other interests."

"I just want you to understand how I operate, Max," said Simon.

"So, it's Max already."

"I take care of people."

"You also lie, Mr. Blake. All you could do with this building is co-op it and the first thing the tenants would do is get rid of me."

"There would be a management clause!" said Simon.

"No, Mr. Blake. The three tenants who would possibly buy their units would insist on no management clause. They're all lawyers."

"Binney told you that I was coming?"

"He called me this morning at home. He said a wise guy named Simon Blake was coming over, don't tell him anything. So, I'm not telling you anything. Actually, I'll tell you anything except what you really want to know. Who owns the building? I don't know who owns the building."

"Do you own it?"

"Blake, if I owned the building I would have sold it years ago. Probably much too soon to make any real money. That's why I sit in this little office and you own the world."

"One eighth of one percent would be more like it," said Simon not sure if he was trying to be funny or sarcastic.

"Congratulations! Then the building isn't going to make one bit of a difference is it? Don't waste your time. And, you know something, in my opinion, Judge Binney owns the building."

"No," said Simon, "he doesn't have enough money."

"Come on, Mr. Blake. Not enough money? A leading jurist, a lawyer, an associate of the great? Not enough money?"

"What does that mean? He's still not worth more than a million and even if he is, he's not stupid enough to stick any of it into a rent controlled building on the West side."

"May I ask you a simple question Mr. Blake? You have much more than a million dollars. Why are you bothering?"

"Quite frankly just because I saw the original."

"Really?" replied Geisler in German. "What original? Why would they copy such an ugly building?"

"I'm not German," said Simon in English.

"But you understand me," said Geisler, again in German. "I suspected you would."

"I was over there during the war," replied Simon. "I supposed you were there, too," he added with a tone of apology.

"I was born in Munich," said Geisler.

"Sorry!"

"You don't have to be, it wasn't your fault what happened." He attempted to re-light his cigar.

Simon reached across his desk and handed him a fresh one.

"Thank you," said Geisler. "What happened, did you suddenly get guilt feelings because you blew up half of Munich?"

"I would have if I had the chance, but when I arrived there the war was over.

"It was on Widenmayer Street. I lived not too far from there."

Simon indicated one of the posters on the wall. "Were you in the movies?"

"And the theater!" said Geisler sticking to his native tongue. "An actor. Only I'm not so effective in English as I was in German and at one point I decided that I didn't want to work in Germany anymore."

"Who owns the building? I'll make it worth your while," said Simon. "Why the mystery?"

"The mystery is," said Geisler, "that I am speaking to you in German and you're understanding every word that I say yet you're answering me in English."

"I studied German in high school."

"I don't buy that!"

"My parents spoke Yiddish."

"I'll buy that," said Geisler. After a pause long enough to light the fresh cigar, he said in English, "Then what's this compulsion to buy the building?"

"Never mind," said Simon. "I'll find the owner on my own."

"It still won't do you any good," said Geisler.

"You wouldn't want to bet on that," said Simon as he rose and hurried out of the office.

## 3

Max Geisler sat for a while enjoying the cigar and trying to figure Simon out. That man couldn't have seen the building. It was a bomb crater when Munich was occupied.

He came to the conclusion that Simon was too good a businessman to act solely on compulsion and that he had bigger plans than turning the building into a co-operative. He would pay through the nose for it. Max Geisler Number Three decided to by-pass Judge Binney and talk to the Max Geisler Number Two directly. He would then give Simon a few days to bang his head against a stone wall before calling on him in person and demanding the entire brokerage fee. He thought, *I've been sitting in this office long enough. It's time for me to retire.*

*Call Max Two?* thought Geisler. *It's against regulations.* Geisler laughed and said aloud, "Regulations? Forty years and still regulations? Who cares anymore?"

# 4

When Simon returned to his own office, he found Art Norman seated behind his desk glancing through a file folder.

"Taking over already?" asked Simon as he removed his jacket and sat opposite him.

"Just being a dutiful son-in-law," replied Art. "You haven't been heard from since two this morning."

"And you thought that I was dead and couldn't wait to take over. Don't forget that I have a regular son."

"A film-maker," said Art, "not a Realtor."

"He'll wise up."

"Until he does, someone has to watch the shop. We had a date with the New York Telephone Company this afternoon."

"I forgot."

"You forgot? You never forget."

"It wasn't important anyway," said Simon. "I'm working on something else."

"May I remind you that Collins and Blakely notified us that they're moving out of New York lock, stock, and barrel when their lease expires. We're going to be stuck with an empty, thirty-five story office building on Park Avenue."

"We won't be stuck."

"We will if we don't find a prime tenant immediately."

"I told you to keep that building off the market. Rentals are so bad now they have no place to go but up." Simon picked up the telephone on the side table and said into it, "Cathy, the stuff on Three Eighty Nine, please."

"I have it here," said Art.

"Good," said Simon hanging up the telephone and crossing to his desk. "How does it look?"

"I didn't know you were negotiating with the Armanda Collier Foundation?"

"The Armanda Collier Foundation?" asked Simon.

"They own the balance of the block front."

"Good. I may want to talk to them," said Simon.

"May?"

"I'm having trouble tracking down the real owner of Three Eighty Nine."

"I would think you'd want to secure the major portion of the assemblage first."

"Assemblage?"

Art noticed that Simon wasn't quite paying attention to him. He hesitated before asking, "Last week, when we had dinner at your house, you talked about going heavily into residential. A big project with Federal funding."

"I just want Three Eighty Nine!" replied Simon.

"What for?"

"Twenty years ago I would have pissed in my pants if I got a hold of a deal like that. Don't knock it."

"Simon, we have a billion dollar plus business to run here. You tied up the entire office staff today running down that building for you. You could have turned it over to a broker and got it over and done within five minutes."

"It's important."

"One little, rent controlled building?"

"As far as I'm concerned it's *the* Project in the office." Simon knew he wasn't making any sense, but the last person in the world he wanted to explain himself to was his son-in-law.

Art handed him the file folder and said, "It's all yours," and started out of the office.

"Wait a minute," said Simon. "You just gave me a look as if I were crazy."

"I don't know. I truthfully don't know," said Art. "You have a knack for making money, I don't. Maybe I'm just not smart."

"You were smart enough to marry my daughter," said Simon sharply.

"Of course. I planned it that way for years in advance," said Art as he swung about, sharply tensing himself for a shouting match. "Are you going to start picking on me again? Not today, Simon!"

"Who says you had to work here? Why don't you try it out on the street first just like I did?"

"Because your daughter has expensive tastes," said Art.

"Does she pick out all you five hundred dollar suits?"

"One of these days, just one of these days, Simon, I may take a walk."

"What will you do?" asked Simon.

"Practice law. If you remember I happen to be a member of the New York bar."

"I'll remember that," said Simon, "if you remember who put you through law school."

"I'll be in my office if you need me!"

As Art turned and left the room, Simon chuckled. Nothing relaxed him more than baiting his son-in-law. He thought, "Look at that bastard, five hundred dollar suits and he never was in the army. How the hell he stayed out of Vietnam, I'll never know." Simon took the file folder to the couch with him and studied its contents looking for a clue to the owner of the building. A memo written by one of his employees read, "389 West 83rd Street was constructed by the firm of Abelard and Abelard (no longer in existence) in 1924 and designed by the architectural firm of Strook, Latham, and Company (no longer in existence). There is no record of any construction loans and the parcel was never mortgaged out. The present owner holds it free and clear. The parcel hasn't changed hands since the 'Three Eighty Nine Corporation' purchased it from the Astor Estate in 1923. The 'Three Eighty Nine Corporation' can be reached c/o the law firm of Cabot, Stiles, Rothschild, and Binney, 350 Park Avenue.

"The managing agent of the building is Max Geisler, 2037 Broadway. I have enclosed various copies of M.B.A. documents, a rent roll, and other papers on said parcel that were on file with the city. I've also had our service run down recent litigation (at rush rates) and the report is insignificant, only minor landlord-tenant disputes. The building has been well maintained and the only recent violations against it are debatable. Since the net income of the building is less than 7% of the market value I would recommend it to someone trying to co-op it only, and only if the property can be obtained at the right price. The efforts may still not be worth the rewards. Certainly not for our company.... Jake."

A knock at the door brought Simon to his feet. He shouted, "Come in."

"It's Morris," said a soft voice on the other side almost apologetically.

"God damn it, Captain! Come on in!" replied Simon.

His old company commander, Morris Ankhorn, a stocky, bent, red-faced man holding his years badly entered slowly. His neatly tailored suit and expensive Swiss shoes seemed to be on the wrong body. "You left a note on my desk?"

"Are you just getting into the office?" asked Simon.

Morris nodded.

Simon said, "It's after four o'clock."

"I wasn't feeling well this morning," replied Morris as he limped over to a chair opposite the couch and sunk into it.

"You were out drinking again! You know what the doctors told you." Simon sat back down.

"They've been telling me that for twenty years."

"Well.... go ahead," said Simon, pointing with his thumb to the section of wall paneling that hid his bar.

"Not now."

"Go ahead!"

"You worry about me too much."

"I'd rather have you get a drink now than have you jiggle for ten minutes trying to con me out of one."

"Thanks!" said Morris. He rose and went to the wall and slid back the panel to expose the bar. "How about you, Simon?"

"Of course! At least I have one friend to drink with in the office."

"You got lots of friends. You're one of the most well liked men in the business."

"Bullshit, all I see around here are a lot of blank faces, and day by day, they're all getting to look more like my son-in-law."

"He thinks you're going crazy," said Morris as he bent down with difficulty to reach into the icemaker. "Something about an old, rent controlled building on the West side. But I set him straight."

"How, Morris?"

"I told him what you were really up to. The assembly of the whole block. That you obviously were making a deal with the Armanda Collier Foundation."

"That wasn't his idea?"

"No, mine. I was thinking about trying it myself years ago."

"And I thought that bastard finally had an idea of his own for once."

Simon picked up the telephone and said into it, "Would you get the son-in-law in here immediately!" He then rose and crossed to the bar. "If I just wanted to buy that building, would it sound crazy?"

"Certainly," said Morris. His hands shook as he poured scotch into Simon's glass. "It's a project for a small time operator. People would look at you with goo-goo eyes if it ever got out."

"What if I just felt like owning it?"

"Like a hobby?" asked Morris putting the scotch down and pouring himself a shot of bourbon whiskey with unsteady hands.

"Like a hobby!" said Simon returning to the couch with his drink.

"Simon Blake isn't allowed any hobbies," said Morris.

"I had a couple in my time. The yacht for one."

"You aren't allowed any real estate hobbies. No one collects old buildings. Now, if you put up a museum or an opera house…"

"Morris, you're right. You're always right! As far as the world is concerned I'm buying the whole block front."

"You are, aren't you?"

"As far as you and I are concerned, no! Sit down and tell me about Three Eighty Nine West Eighty-third Street."

Morris made his way to a chair opposite Simon carefully carrying his drink. As he sat he said, "The *Englischer Garten*. Strange?"

Simon nodded.

"Built in the turn-of-the-century style just as the market was shifting into art deco and neo-modern." Morris took a sip of his drink and lapsed into silence. One would think that he was about to fall asleep.

"It's a twin of another building," said Simon loudly. He was going to mention Munich, but he decided to let Morris discover for himself the fact that they had both seen the other building before.

Morris didn't take the hint. He said, "Strange for a parcel in New York that old. The same family holding onto it so long. From day one as it were."

"Family?" asked Simon.

"I assume as much!" said Morris taking another sip of his drink.

Art entered, slamming the door behind. He shouted at Simon, "Will you stop referring to me as the son-in-law? How about just plain son-in-law for a change?"

"Look who's talking," said Simon. "The liar."

"Liar?" shouted Art.

"Taking another man's ideas. Morris thought of assembling the whole block."

"I never said I conceived the idea. I thought it was what you were up to."

"Get yourself a drink and sit down."

"It's almost five. I promised my wife I'd be home early today."

"We're having a business meeting."

"I promised Karen."'

"If she gives you a hard time tell her about all the times she kept her family waiting."

"May I have a drink?"

"I just told you to take one." He turned back to Morris and asked, "Tell my son-in-law here what you know about the building."

Another long pause and then Morris replied, "The title isn't clear."

"How did you first come across the building?" asked Simon.

"I knew one of the tenants. A woman there."

"Mrs. Rosenthal?" said Simon glancing at the rent role.

"I don't remember her name."

"Think, Morris!" said Simon. "You saw that building long before you ever met Mrs. Rosenthal."

"No, I didn't spend any time in New York until after the war," said Morris with half closed eyes.

"Nineteen Forty Five," said Art. "I was born exactly nine months after my father got back from Guam."

"We all know the date, and Morris's war didn't end then. He stayed on in Europe as a prosecutor at Nuremberg."

"Assistant prosecutor," said Morris with a yawn.

"He arrested Otto Skorzeny."

"I didn't arrest him. I took testimony from him in Spain. Quite an interesting fellow. Likable!" Morris rose shakily to his feet. "I'd like to go now."

"Sure, Morris," said Simon. "Take it easy. There's only one thing I want you to do for me in the morning. See if the plans are still on file for Three Eighty Nine."

After Morris left, Art said, "Take it easy? All he does in his office is sleep. That is, when he comes in."

"He's worth his weight in gold," said Simon crossing to the bar to refresh his drink. "He knew all about the building." He pointed to the file folder he had left on the couch. "You didn't have to pay for all that info. You could have just asked Morris."

"He's drawing well over a thousand dollars a week. For what?"

"For being my friend, kiddo. For being a combat soldier. For being my company commander in World War Two. One thing they'll never say about Simon Blake in this town is that he forgot."

"We're not running a charity here."

"We're not running anything. I'm running. And I don't want to hear another word against Morris. He almost owned a third of this company. He had a lot of money once. He almost bought in."

## 5

Morris returned to his office, opened a desk drawer, and took out a bottle of bourbon from which he poured a drink into a paper cup. His mind was clearing against his wishes. He kept on hearing Simon repeating, "Get me the plans for Three Eight Nine" and he was well aware that Simon was trying to get him to mention the building's twin in Munich. "He knows. He must have known all along. He couldn't have just stumbled on that building by accident. But why did he wait all these years? Why is he starting to play games with me? The twin in Munich? Simon never saw the twin in Munich! It was flattened. That would have been impossible." He thought, *Oh, God, the picture on the mantelpiece in Steinhoffen.*

## 6

Simon made sure that he was late for his appointment with Ray Warren so that the tall, slender, graying lawyer had to wait on the corner of Eighty-Third Street for ten minutes before he arrived. As Ray hurried up to the Cadillac, Simon lowered the window and shouted, "Ray, old buddy!"

Ray replied, "What's this with meeting on street corners? What was I supposed to do, count the cracks in the sidewalk?"

"You could have looked at the pretty girls."

"A, I'm too old for pretty girls. B, I didn't see any."

"What else did you see?" asked Simon.

"Nothing!"

"Nothing!" Simon couldn't believe that Ray hadn't recognized the building. "Are you sure?"

"Simon, I'm not going to play games no matter how much I love you. What was I supposed to see?"

"The building!" There was elation in Simon's voice.

"Which one?"

"The one you're standing in front of."

"So?" asked Ray glancing over his shoulder.

"Look carefully."

With a sigh, Ray turned and looked up at three eighty-nine. "Okay, what next?"

"Get in the car!"

Ray stepped around to the passenger side of the Seville and slid into the seat next to Simon. "Simon, you're still as crazy as ever. Let's go get a drink."

"Don't you recognize the building?"

"No!"

"You've seen it before," said Simon as he joined traffic for the short trip to the bar.

"I'm sure I've seen it before," answered Ray by the time they parked again and got out. "I lived three blocks from it once. I used to walk a big, dumb dog three times a day. That was the big mistake of my life."

"What?" asked Simon.

"The dog and my second wife. Hey wait a second! You took me to a party in that building in Nineteen Fifty. Three roommates. Actresses. What's the big deal?"

"It was before that," said Simon.

"Before that? The last time I saw you before that was in Europe."

"You saw the building in Germany."

"What did it do? Book passage on Pam Am, or swim over here?"

"It's a duplicate of a building we saw in Munich," said Simon as he waved a waitress over to put in a drink order.

"I still don't remember," said Ray. "And, if I saw anything so obviously middle class I would have torn it apart with cannon fire. You know how I felt about the krauts."

"A billet," asked Simon. "Besides the war was over when we hit Munich."

"We never billeted in a place that looked like that in Munich."

"I remember going into a building just like it. On Widenmayer Street. Hey, I know, that was where those two cute *frauleins* lived."

"Greta and Ingrid," said Ray.

"Right!" said Simon.

"Wrong! They lived in Schwabbing.

"On the river," insisted Simon.

"In Schwabbing," shouted Ray happily. "I went back to see them in Forty Eight."

"And?"

"I told you about it. Greta had married a G.I. I fooled around with Ingrid for a couple of days."

"Ingrid was in love with me."

"She was only in love with your cigarettes. Let's have another shot."

"I have to buy that building!" said Simon.

"Today?" asked Ray.

"Fate!" replied Simon holding his already-empty glass up in sight of the waitress for a refill. "I feel as if I was destined to find that building again."

"You mean, I wouldn't have to listen to all this if your daughter came home early and didn't piss you off?"

"There's more to it than that," said Simon handing Ray a file folder he had brought in with him.

"Okay! You saw the building in Munich and now you want to bring it home. Like the Luger you picked up off the SS officer you shot." Ray pushed the file folder back to Simon. "I don't want to talk about business tonight."

"If you had talked about business when I wanted you to, you have been a rich man today."

"I did okay."

"What happened to all your money?"

"Three wives."

"I'm giving you another chance," said Simon pointing to the file folder. "Partners?"

"I'm afraid I'm not in a position to buy a building at the moment."

"I'll lay out your end."

"No thanks," said Ray. "I can take care of myself."

"How?"

"I get a pension and a salary."

"Peanuts."

"I'm practicing law full time. Thirty years too late, but I'm practicing."

"For a government agency. What kind of law is that?"

"I can take care of myself. I don't want to wind up like Morris. He's always been a schmuck."

"Don't say that! He was an excellent officer and a brilliant attorney."

"Yeah, maybe," he shrugged. "I would have never gone to law school after the war if it weren't for him. And if it weren't for women and booze he would be sitting on the Supreme Court today."

"How about," asked Simon. "How about if I retain you to handle the purchase of the building for me?" He placed the file folder on Ray's side of the table. "I'll also arrange a co-brokerage fee for you."

"I'm not a real estate lawyer."

"You're my friend. It doesn't matter."

"I'm not a member of the New York bar."

"You know something," said Simon, "you're the only guy I know who lies to avoid making money.

Ray put the book back on Simon's side of the table. Simon said, "I need your investigative ability."

"What investigative ability?" asked Art.

"Thirty years with the C.I.A."

"Whoever told you I worked for the C.I.A.?"

"*The New York Times!*" said Simon.

"Simon, I wasn't an investigator. I wasn't cloak and dagger. I was an administrator."

"That's not what *The New York Times* said," laughed Simon. He drummed his fingers on the file folder. "Find me the owner of that building and I'll see that you're the lawyer of record at the closing."

"That's charity, Simon. The owner of the building is the Three Eighty Nine West Eighty-third Street Corporation. It's right in the file."

"I want to know the stockholders."

Ray took up the file and opened it. Immediately, he poked a finger at one of the pages. "Have your secretary call Cabot, Stiles, Rothschild, and Binney."

"Judge Binney refuses to put me in touch with the principals. There's some hanky-panky."

"Why? I heard he was a pretty nice guy."

"A stuck up, old bastard."

"Not from what I heard. He was with the OSS during the war. He lost two sons. One at Pearl and another over Holland. If you shoot straight with him, he'll shoot straight with you."

"Then why is he trying to jiggle me?"

Ray took a deep breath and said, "I'll see what I can do. These blind corporations can be ball busters."

"Then you know where to start looking?"

"I think so!" said Ray, finally discovering what he was looking for in the file. "Max Geisler! Law firms like Cabot, Stills, Rothschild, and Binney don't usually deal with refugees in walk-up offices on upper Broadway. Let me talk to him."

# 7

There was a young, New York City policeman sitting in a chair outside of Geisler's office smoking a cigarette against regulations. He rose as Simon and Ray approached and asked, "Can I help you gentlemen?"

Simon replied, "Is Max Geisler in there?"

"Yup!" said the officer.

"We'd like to talk to him."

"That would be very difficult, sir," said the young officer. "He's dead."

"Dead?" asked Simon. "What happened?"

"He was murdered this afternoon."

"Murdered?"

"Probably some junkie. It happens every day in this neighborhood."

"I'm his partner," said Simon stepping forward. "I have to get some papers out of the office."

"I'm sorry, but I can't let anyone in but the Medical Examiner."

"It's important!" Simon reached for the money clip in his pocket.

"Sorry!" said the young police officer. Ray took Simon by the shoulder and practically pulled him back down the stairs. When they reached the street, Simon said, "We have to find out who killed Geisler!"

"Why?" asked Ray. "It was just a robbery."

"Not just a robbery! He was killed to keep me from getting my hands on that building!" said Simon loud enough to attract the attention of people on the street. "We've got to go over to the precinct house

"Not right now," said Ray. "You're letting this whole thing get out of hand. Go home and get a good night's sleep and I'll work on it first thing in the morning."

"I won't be able to sleep!" shouted Simon. "I want that building!"

"Simon, don't you know you're acting irrationally?" said Ray softly.

"Am I?" asked Simon.

"Yes!" said Ray.

"Let's go out and get drunk."

# 8

Simon was awoken by the noise the maid made in his bathroom. He turned his head to the side and tried to read the time on the face of the miniature, antique clock on the night table. It was impossible. His wife, Gilda, had gone through an interior decorating phase, including a course at the New School for Social Research, and she refused to allow a modern clock radio in the master bedroom as it clashed with the French decor. He called out, "Norma! What time is it?"

"Eleven, Mr. Blake," replied the maid.

Simon rose, slipped on a robe, and went into the bath where he found the maid scouring the tub. He said, "Do you mind?"

She answered, "I'm cleaning in here."

"You don't have to. I haven't used it since you cleaned it yesterday."

The maid, ignoring him, said, "Use Mrs. Blake's."

"There's no phone in there! Out!" growled Simon. After the maid left reluctantly, Simon sat down to relieve himself, at the same time dialing the ivory telephone on the wall. When his office in New York answered, he said, "This is Mr. Blake. I'd like to speak to Mr. Ankhorn."

"Who?" asked the operator.

"Morris!"

"Oh, Morris! He's not in yet," said the operator.

Simon next dialed Morris's home number. The phone wasn't picked up until the tenth ring. A sleepy, girlish voice came on and said, "Hello?"

"Put Morris on, honey!" said Simon impatiently.

"He's still sleeping."

"He's drunk," shouted Simon into the telephone. "Put him on!" There was silence for a moment and then Morris got on the phone and said, "Simon?"

"You were supposed to go downtown and get those plans for me."

"Talk to the girl," said Morris.

Simon shouted, "Morris, I don't want to talk to a hooker. I—"

When the girl's voice came on again, Simon hung up.

He entered the breakfast room, glanced at the food on the table, and asked Gilda, "Where's Ray?"

"After he carried you up to bed last night, he drove back to the city."

"At four o'clock in the morning?" asked Simon. Gilda nodded. Simon looked down at the table and then asked, "Who is the other place setting for?"

"Your son!"

"The film-maker?" asked Simon.

"You only have one son. Or did you forget?" said Gilda.

"Would you be a honey and call the Taft Hotel and get Ray on the phone for me?"

"He called an hour ago, Simon. He isn't at the hotel. He'll call you back."

Simon's son Sam came down the stairs and entered the breakfast room clad in jeans and a T-shirt. Simon quipped, "The beard has arrived."

"Good morning, Mom," said Sam ignoring his father completely.

"I thought you were working as an assistant editor? Fifty bucks a week. That was pretty good money in Eighteen Seventy Five."

"He quit," said Gilda.

"I'm busy with an article for Films in Review. The Hungarian Cinema in the Thirties."

"How much are they going to pay you?" asked Simon.

"The money doesn't matter. It's just what I happen to be interested in at the moment." Sam yawned.

"Are you going down to the city today?" asked Simon.

"To the library."

"How about going downtown and getting me a set of plans on an old building for me. You've done it before."

"You have people at the office for that."

"I only have one son."

"I'll be too busy," said Sam with a patronizing sigh as he buttered his toast

"Fifty bucks? A whole weeks pay!" said Simon with a sadistic laugh.

"No," said Sam.

"I just met a guy with a whole collection of old German movie stills and posters," said Simon thinking quickly. "He just kicked the bucket. You can pick up the lot for a song."

"Reproductions?"

"Originals!" said Simon not having any idea what he was talking about. "Run down and get the plans and I'll set you up."

"What's the address of the building?" asked Sam.

The telephone in the kitchen rang. Simon beat Gilda to it and picked it up to hear Ray Warren say, "Hello?"

Simon replied, "What did you find out?"

"I spoke to Homicide North. It was obviously a robbery. The place was ransacked."

"Did you ever think they were searching for something?" said Simon.

"Like what?"

"Anything with the names of the stockholders on it."

"It was a junkie, Simon. You're building this into something it isn't."

"Just for fun, let's take a look in Geisler's office tonight."

"Why?" asked Ray. You just said the place was searched for the very thing you're looking for."

"And you just said it was nothing but a robbery. If you're right, then Geisler may have something in his files."

"Simon, you're talking about breaking and entering."

"If you're scared, I'll do it myself."

"Fine, but I'll speak to the Judge first."

# 9

Ray had always been impressed by Simon's house, but when he entered Judge Binney's office he was awe struck. Its walls were entirely paneled in black oak and overhead was a beamed ceiling that encroached on the head space of the floor above. It stood above a working fireplace which held on its mantle a photograph of each of Binney's long dead sons in uniform and one of his late wife, the boys' mother, when she was very young. Ray was so taken in by the extreme good taste of the room, that it was moments before his eyes settled on the ram rod stiff figure of the Judge standing by the Renaissance dining table that served as his desk. Binney had a cat-like smile on his face. He asked, "Like the decor?"

"I'm speechless."

"War loot," said the Judge. He pointed to a painting of a French Chateau above his desk. "I was billeted there during the war. Fell in love with the study. Took the whole thing back home with me. Never got caught!" After studying Ray for a moment he said, "A friend of the rich and powerful. How is young Cyrus?"

"Young?" said Ray.

"To me he's young. Ray Warren is it? I recall reading something about you in *The New York Times*. Did Jane Fonda ever put you in jail?"

"I'm standing here," said Ray.

"Well, sit down!"

Ray took a seat and said, "I don't want to take up too much of your time."

"Why not? I have enough. I've had eighty-five years so far. That's a lot longer than most men. Say hello to Parri. I'm at an age when I need a full time nurse maid again. Parri's a retired Navy Chief. I told him it wasn't a job for a man, but he insists on taking care of me."

Ray turned to discover a young man with a crew cut standing near the judge. "Retired?" asked Ray with disbelief.

"In at seventeen and out at thirty-seven," said Parri with a respectful smile.

"Did you start with the OSS?" the Judge asked Ray.

"No, I was a combat officer during the war. I came out of it a First Lieutenant."

"Airborne?" asked the Judge.

"No," said Ray. "Armored!"

"Shermans?"

"All the way," said Ray.

The Judge turned to Parri and said, "I could use a cigar, and give one to the tanker, too."

Parri brought a teak humidor to the Judge and after he selected a cigar, brought it to Ray and asked, "Would you like some coffee?"

Ray took the cigar and said, "I'm sure the Judge has another appointment."

"It can wait," said Judge Binney. "Have some coffee."

"Okay," said Ray. Parri snapped the humidor closed, placed it back on the sideboard, and then handed Ray a silver cigar clipper that the Judge had passed to him. After

Parri lit the cigar for Ray, the Judge said, "Parri is very servile for a Walrus."

"I think you mean Seal," said Ray. "Sea .... Air .... Land."

"The judge knows," Parri assured him. "He's just kidding."

"I assume you were forced into retiring," said the Judge. Ray nodded. The Judge continued, "Are you double dipping now?"

"With the Department of the Interior. I have a law degree but I never really practiced."

The Judge motioned to Parri who took up a steno pad and sat ready to take dictation.

"That's not necessary, sir," said Ray.

"Yes it is!" said the Judge. "A young man came up here looking for a job in television and I had him placed in a bank. My memory isn't as good as it used to be."

Ray said, "Simon Blake was up to see about a building."

"No!" said the Judge leaning back in his chair. "I can't stand the man. One of those people with nothing on his mind but money. Never did anything that didn't lead to his own enrichment."

"Not true!" said Ray strongly. "He was one of my tank commanders during the war. He was awarded the Silver Star and he still hasn't forgotten any of the guys in our outfit. I think he's done more for our division than the Veteran's Administration. And you can believe I'm here to do him a favor. I expect no compensation."

"Silver Star?"

"And wounded twice."

"Well, young man, tell me what the hell he wants that lousy building for? The Armanda Collier Trust owns the rest of the block and there's no way they can sell. Her will states so clearly and I should know, I drew it up—" The Judge stopped talking suddenly and looked as if someone had just slapped him in the face. He said, "Twelfth Armored Division? You boys occupied Munich. You came south through ....?"

"Steinhoffen!" said Ray. "That was the end of it for us. The last battle. But, how did you know it was the Twelfth Armored?"

"What the hell are you playing games for?" shouted the Judge.

"I don't understand?" said Ray.

"You're playing games! Parri, show this man out"

"I don't understand," said Ray.

The Judge snapped at Parri, "Out!"

## 10

The moment he was alone, the Judge started to cry. He wiped his eyes with his breast pocket handkerchief and thought, "Why, after all these years?"

He left the office and took the stairs down to the Fortieth floor where he grabbed a young associate by the arm and pulled him into a records storage room. He said, "There's a corporate kit in here someplace. Help me find it. My eyes aren't too good anymore. It's titled the Three Eighty Nine West Eighty-third Street Corporation."

It took the young lawyer an hour to locate it. He dusted it off for the Judge and placed it on a library table. Turning to the shares issued section of the stock book, the Judge thought, *I shouldn't have blown up like that. I could have been wrong.*

He took out his pocket magnifier and bent close to the page he wanted. The last entries in his own handwriting read, "One share issued to Cpt. Ankhorn, Morris, 4/30/45... One share issued to Lt. Warren, Ray, 4/30/45... One share issued to T. Sgt. Blake, Simon, 4/30/45."

# 11

Judge Binney was an overage, National Guard Colonel who used every political connection he had, including the President himself, to wrangle a combat command and was preparing for the jump across the Rhine when he was ordered back to Washington on the highest priority. As he returned to the United States he was sure that he was being "saved" by friends in high places for a post-war political post.

He had guessed wrong. He was driven directly from the airport to a nondescript office in Washington, D.C. to confront Wild Bill Donavan who informed him that he was about to make a contribution to the war effort in league with the Office of Strategic Services that would overshadow anything he could contribute as an airborne infantry officer.

Donavan said, "You may be responsible for shortening the war by at least a year."

"How?" asked Binney.

"I can't disclose that now." Donavan put his arm around Binney's shoulders and started easing him towards the door.

It wasn't until Binney was assigned a tutor and ordered to brush up on his German that he realized that they had found "the woman" again. "The woman" that he had spent so many years searching for. Feeling safe enough to expose herself, she had asked that he and only he be sent to Germany to make a deal with her because he was the only man in the world that she could trust and she was positive that he would not jeopardize his military mission in order to extract personal vengeance.

## 12

In the distance, Simon saw an imposing structure. It was completely enclosed with glass so that the center mast that held it suspended above the landscape was completely visible making it appear that the building was still waiting to be lowered onto its site thirty years after its construction. Simon slowed down so that he would not miss the sign, which read, "Exit 72 - Collier Forest."

He flipped on his directional signal, turned off the highway, and then followed a series of smaller signs through the pines that read, "Administration Building — Visitors Parking." The road narrowed as he continued upward and Simon thought that he had made a wrong turn until he spotted still another sign in a bit of a clearing to his right. He turned onto an even narrower road, designed to preserve the second growth stand of New England forest, and found himself entering a parking garage deep in a hill underneath the suspended structure. He got out of the Cadillac, locked it, and entered a waiting elevator.

When its doors opened on the Reception Level, Simon was greeted by a spectacular view of the Connecticut Valley that he had just driven through, framed by the bare, steel beams girding the tinted window wall. "Hi!" said a young man in a sports shirt who rose from behind a plain metal desk set to one side of the elevator. "Can I help you, sir?"

"I have an appointment with Mr. Dennis," said Simon getting a kick out of the pretentious informality of it all.

The young man glanced down at an appointment book. "Mr. Blake?"

Simon nodded.

"If you continue on straight ahead, you'll find Mr. Dennis on the left at the far end of the level."

Simon thanked the young man and continued on in the direction he had indicated, traversing a huge, quiet, executive area, divided only by waist high partitions, and found Dennis in a far corner, rising to greet him as he approached. Simon said, "Mr. Dennis?"

Dennis, a rather thinnish man in a somber, gray suit with seemingly premature, gray hair, stepped away from his desk, shook hands with Simon, and then indicated a seat on a couch set against a partition.

"Please, I hope you don't mind the lack of privacy. There is no such thing as a private office here at the Collier Foundation."

"What happened?" asked Simon as he made himself comfortable. "Did some management maven sell you a bill of goods?"

"No, the old lady hated private offices. They prevented her from keeping an eye on her employees. No private offices, no interior walls. It's all in her will along with the provision forbidding us from selling that property on West Eighty-Third Street."

"Then why did you invite me out?" asked Simon.

Dennis lowered his voice to a whisper. "The old guard's gone now. I think our current board of directors would be in the mood to find a way to beat that stipulation.

Any funds realized from the sale can be put to much better use. There's no need to tell you that those brownstones are being run at a loss."

"Have you tried renovating?" said Simon. "They're getting some pretty good rents on that side of town these days."

"The old lady broke them into small apartments in her day and we're prohibited from making any further structural changes."

"I would have to acquire the apartment building on the corner to complete the package," said Simon getting to his real reason for the long drive out.

"Judge Binney will sell," said Dennis. "That is if the old coot is still alive. I haven't spoken to him in years."

"He's very much alive," replied Simon. "He says he doesn't own the building."

"It's all a matter of public record."

"Not the stockholders of the Three Eighty Nine Corporation."

Dennis slipped into thought for a moment. He then said, "I shouldn't tell you this, but, then again, it's all a matter of public record."

"Tell me what?" asked Simon.

"Armanda Collier died thinking that she owned that building. That her son built it with funds embezzled from her. That's where Judge Binney comes into the picture. He represented Armanda in her later years and handled all the litigation in her attempt to recover the parcel. His efforts were unsuccessful. But shortly after her death, he ended up in control of the building. That was bit unethical, don't you think? I mean he represented Armanda. Why, he even drew up her will and was an original director of this foundation."

"Who did they sue?" asked Simon.

"The corporation, but they could never prove that her son was connected with it in any way. It's all on record. A young woman wrote a most sensational interpretation of Armanda's life a little while back. It shouldn't be difficult to come by a copy. I believe it's called, 'Lady Midas.' The author's name is Jane Scott."

"Do I have to read an entire book to find out who you think owns the building?"

"That's all I can do to help you. This foundation exists only until Collier or any of the heirs turn up. It's that way in the will."

"I can see why you guys aren't in too much of a hurry to find the stockholders of the Three Eighty Nine Corporation."

"Not in any more of a hurry than they are to be found. I think you may have to build around that apartment building."

"No way," said Simon.

"Then I wish you the best of luck! How about lunch? We have a rather nice dining room on the Senior Level."

"Senior Level?"

"The old lady didn't like floors either," said Dennis as he took Simon by the arm and led him to the elevators. They made one stop before entering the executive dining room—the nondenominational chapel which contained the only two pieces of art work in the building. A bronze bust of Armanda Collier engraved "October 2nd, 1873 - January 3rd, 1929" and a bronze bust of Crowell C. Collier engraved, "April 20th, 1889."

## 13

As they walked up the ramp of the parking garage, Ray said, "Simon, are you crazy? You're not a burglar."

"Right. All I want to do is take a look in Geisler's office."

"What do you expect to find in there?"

"The owner of my building."

"There are other ways to do this. It's not worth getting arrested for."

"We won't get arrested. It's all arranged," said Simon, hurrying ahead of Ray.

## 14

Irving Pitchnik waited in front of the Broadway building he owned wearing his best overcoat. Pitchnik, a thin faced man of sixty who had never seen better days, had walked all the way up and over from his apartment on Central Park West to do Simon Blake a favor, because big or small, if you operated real estate in New York City, you rushed to the telephone like a fool when Blake called, especially when you thought yourself smart enough to assume why Simon Blake wanted to look in Max Geisler's office.

Pitchnik assumed, hopefully, that Blake had no interest in the talkative refugee's belongings and just using the murder victim as an excuse to get a closer look at the property before making an offer. *Of course*, thought Pitchnik, *I'll get the two million I've been holding out for*. Pitchnik had been holding out for two million dollars for so many years that he forgotten what he planned to do with the money if anybody ever paid it to him.

## 15

"That's Pitchnik, the big operator," said Simon nudging Ray as they walked up.

Pitchnik nodded and shook hands with Simon and Ray, whom he also smiled for on the assumption that Ray was an appraiser.

Simon asked, "Pitchnik, did you bring the keys?"

"Of course! Now tell me what's so interesting about Geisler's office?"

"He's my uncle!" replied Simon. Ray bit his lip as Pitchnik's dream of a quick, two million dollar sales quickly faded. Pitchnik asked, "I thought Max was alone in the world? He lost everybody in the camps."

"Actually, he's an uncle of mine, once removed," said Simon lying artfully.

The answer satisfied Pitchnik. It also resolved the matter of Geisler's funeral arrangements and the matter of clearing out the office so that the space could be re-rented immediately.

As they entered the lobby of Pitchnik's building, Simon said, "Did you ever think of keeping this door locked and installing a buzzer system? It's the law! Maybe Geisler would still be alive."

"Who can afford a buzzer system? You know, more than anybody else, what fuel oil costs today."

"Yeah, yeah," said Simon taking the steps two at a time. "Pitchnik's a big operator," he said to Ray. "What have you got now Pitchnik? Two buildings?"

"One and a half. My brother-in-law owns the other half, but he's never around when you need him."

"Get him to paint the hall."

"You can't collect rent on the hall," answered Pitchnik.

"Pitchnik, you really know how to make a buck." Simon stopped in front of Geisler's door and said, "Open it up."

Pitchnik stepped in front of Simon, unlocked the door, and held it open. Simon and Ray entered the darkened reception room. Pitchnik followed, shutting the door behind, and then turning on the overhead lights, he said to Simon, "I suppose you gave him the Eighty Third Street building to manage so he wouldn't starve to death?"

"He got it on his own. You don't know who owns that building, do you?" asked Simon.

"He never mentioned an owner," said Pitchnik as Ray cleared a space to sit, picked up a movie magazine and glanced through it. Pitchnik continued, "He liked people to think that he was the owner. He used to spend all his money on young girls. He didn't stop after the prostate operation."

Simon started with the top, center drawer of the desk. It contained a checkbook and the building's ledger. He didn't want Pitchnik to note his interest in it so he continued on to one of the side drawers. It contained a chess set, a cup full of pennies, a variety of office supplies, and some more movie magazines. Pitchnik said, "It's not in there."

"How do you know? You haven't the slightest idea of what I'm looking for."

"The insurance policy."

"I'm not interested in his insurance policy."

"You have to show it to the undertaker if you don't want to pay cash. You're burying him aren't you?"

Simon reached for an answer as Pitchnik continued, "He was your relative, not mine. One sundown passed already. You have to wait till Sunday already."

"Did *you* look for an insurance policy?" asked Ray.

"No insurance policy, no relatives, no veteran's papers, no friends. Just some young shiksas. They don't pay for funerals."

"What about—"

"I looked in his apartment already. No insurance policy. Expensive clothes. No insurance policy. A big color television set. No insurance policy. I called up the medical examiner's office. They released the body to me. Nobody else wants it. I thought I was going to be stuck with the whole thing."

Simon stopped what he was doing and said, "You were going to pay for the funeral?"

"I take care of my tenants," replied Pitchnik.

"I would, too, if I had as few as you," said Simon.

Pitchnik asked, "Did you make any arrangements?"

"Did you?" asked Simon.

"I was debating with my wife. Plots are expensive."

"Have him cremated," say Ray trying to be helpful. "You can get the whole job done for under three hundred dollars."

Pitchnik turned to Ray and said, "No!"

"He wasn't orthodox," said Simon.

"No!" said Pitchnik. "What kind of a nephew are you?"

Ray had to force himself to keep from laughing.

Simon said, "Would you do me a favor, Pitchnik? Go over to Memorial and have them take care of it. Tell them to bill me. Tell them to find the plot. Talk to Kaplan over there."

"How much should I spend?" asked Pitchnik.

"As cheap as possible," replied Simon.

"For your uncle?"

"Two thousand dollars," said Simon and then he got an idea. "Pitchnik, make it three thousand and have them put big memorial ads in the papers."

"A waste of money," said Pitchnik.

"He had a lot of friends you didn't know about," said Simon as Pitchnik reached for the telephone. Simon took Pitchnik's hand off of the phone and said, "Please, Pitchnik, run over there and pick out a nice casket for him."

"A pine box."

"He wasn't that orthodox. Walnut with a Star of David on it. And, please, get a decent Rabbi."

"I'll go make the arrangements," Pitchnik nodded to Ray and then left the office.

Ray rose, yawned, and then said, "This little caper just cost you three grand."

"So what," said Simon. "Someone had to bury the poor guy. He's all alone in the world, and, I bet we get a lead on the owners of the building at the funeral."

"You've been seeing too many movies, buddy boy," laughed Ray as Simon opened the center drawer of the desk again and took out the ledger and checkbook and flipped through their pages quickly. He then took an old fashioned, non-electric machine from the top of one of the file cabinets and started running up a column of figures on the tape. "Ah," he said, "I got an arrow pointing at the real owner."

"Who?" asked Ray, yawning again.

"The building nets around ten thousand a month. Geisler was drawing out all the income except his management fee in cash. The real owners got the cash. Tricky."

An hour later, Simon shut the drawer of the last file cabinet and said, "He's got every piece of paper in this place correctly filed and cross-indexed, but not a clue to the other partners. Not even a check to Binney for legal fees."

Pitchnik let himself in the front door with his key and called out, "It's Pitchnik. I made all the arrangements for Sunday at eleven. They have a plot up in Rockland County. The Rabbi wants you to call him."

"The Rabbi?" asked Simon.

"In case you have anything special you want him to say at the service."

"You take care of that, Pitchnik! Stuff about him losing his family in the Holocaust. The hell he went through in a concentration camp only to be murdered by a punk here."

Pitchnik looked Simon straight in the eye and said, "Are you sure you're related to Max?"

"We weren't very close," said Simon turning quickly to avoid the look he knew was in Ray's eyes. "Why do you ask?"

"He didn't go to a concentration camp. He hid in an apartment in Munich."

## 16

Simon parked blocking the driveway. He left his keys on the hall table so that he wouldn't be awakened if anyone in the family got an earlier start than he. He then went into the den where he flicked on the television set for a restless moment, rose, and tiptoed upstairs to his bedroom, undressing quietly as not to awake his wife who sensed his presence and muttered, "Simon?"

"Sorry!"

"Sam wants to see you," said Gilda groggily. "He went down to the city for you."

"Right. He wants his fifty bucks. Is Charlene home?"

Gilda sat up and pushed the sleep shades off her eyes. "Don't be sarcastic. Of course she's home."

"I was curious. I'm just her father." Simon crossed to the bed and kissed Gilda on the forehead. "You want a cup of coffee?"

"Not at one o'clock in the morning."

"Go back to bed!" Simon put on a pair of pajamas and a robe and went to Sam's door, and, upon hearing the muted television set within, knocked softly. His son replied, "Pop?"

"Are you up?"

"Sure!"

"Can I come in?"

Sam was sprawled across his bed, hypnotized by a late movie. Simon asked him, "Did you get the plans?"

Sam motioned towards his desk.

Simon looked at the plans for a moment, disappointed with the layout of the apartments and noticing a distinct lack of grandeur. He said to Sam, "You've been studying these?"

"The building's interesting. I have a friend that lives there."

"You didn't mention that before."

"I didn't realize it myself until I went over for a look. I like the apartments. The ceilings are low, but they all have two bedrooms." Sam crossed to the desk and handed Simon a yellow, Manila envelope.

The first sheet of paper it contained was a copy of a *New York Times* real estate story dated February 23, 1923.

NEW LUXURY RESIDENCE ON THE WEST SIDE

Clients of Burke, Chaplin, and Morre, have acquired the North West corner of 83rd Street and Riverside Drive from the Astor Estate for the construction of a new, 11 story, luxury apartment building to be erected on the site. Strook, Latham, and Company have been retained as architects.

The second sheet was a copy of a Ripley's "Believe It or Not" box which appeared in the *New York Journal American* in 1948. Below the sketch of an apartment building resembling the one Simon discovered there was the caption, "Monument to a Lost Love.... 389 West 83rd Street, an apartment building in Manhattan, is the exact duplicate of a building on Widenmayer Street in Munich. A German immigrant to the United States spent a fortune to have it match its twin in Bavaria exactly so that his fiancée would feel completely at home when she came to New York to marry him. She never did."

Sam shut off the television and said, "It's not an exact duplicate. The one in Germany is a solid masonry building, built at the turn of the century. The one on Eighty-third has a steel frame and brick curtain walls faced with stone. It's only six stories high. Ripley was wrong. The only thing that matches is the facade and not in detail. The doorway—"

"Right!" said Simon. "The one in Munich had a heavy, oaken door."

"Iron studded," added Sam.

"How do you know so much?" asked Simon.

"I saw the building today."

"The one in Munich?" asked Simon playfully.

"Bernie had a picture of it," yawned Sam.

"Bernie?"

"Bernie Global. My friend that lives in the building. He's a photographer."

"What was he doing with the picture?"

"He's fascinated with the place. He dug it up at the library."

"Does he know who the owner is?"

"Max Geisler."

"Geisler was just the manager."

"You met Max?" asked Sam.

"Once."

"Did you ever see him perform?"

"Perform what?" asked Simon.

Sam pointed to the remaining sheet of paper in Simon's hand. It was a neatly typed carbon copy which read:

"MAX GEISLER (DAVID MOISHE GEISLER)

David Moishe Geisler, born in Munich, Germany on December 5th, 1892, the son of a rabbi, was better known to a generation of Germans as 'Maxi.' A star of both the musical theater and the infant Bavarian film industry, he rose to prominence in a series of motion pictures produced in Munich in the 1920's and was Germany's leading slapstick comedian until 1933. A strong socialist, he was noted for his satirical impersonations of Adolph Hitler and other leaders of the 3rd Reich.

Imprisoned by the Nazis in 1939, he escaped from detention by impersonating a Gestapo officer and went into hiding, spending almost all of World War Two hidden in the closet of a friend's apartment in Munich. Among the films he appeared in were—"

"No, I never saw him perform," said Simon. "How old do you think I am, anyway?"

"Sorry," replied Sam with a shrug. "He was such a good character actor and make-up artist that he used to go out to the cafes in Munich during the war and even though he was a film star, people still wouldn't recognize him."

"Who told you that?"

"Geisler!"

"You met him?"

"He used to hang out in Bernie's apartment. Bernie does portfolios for young actresses and the old man had an eye for them."

"Why didn't he stay an actor? Running one lousy building isn't what I call a career."

"His humor was very regional. Very Bavarian, low and crude .... and, I guess the war did him in. I never heard him crack a joke. All he did was talk about the old days in Germany."

"Where did you get this?" asked Simon holding up the carbon copy.

"Bernie and I wrote it. We thought he deserved a little bit of belated recognition. I took it around to the newspapers this afternoon."

"He's being buried on Sunday. The service is at eleven. Memorial on the West side."

"I didn't know."

"You know now. Be there. I'm paying for the funeral. Now how about coming down to the kitchen. I'll make you a cup of coffee."

"Okay," said Sam. As his father started out of the room he added, "Pop, that was a nice gesture. I bet no one else in the whole world thought about burying Geisler."

"I only hope that you remember when it comes my turn."

Simon put the coffee on then dropped some butter into an omelet pan and turned up the heat under it. When Sam entered the kitchen, Simon said stiffly, "You used to love jelly omelets when you were a kid. I bet you don't even remember?"

"I remember," said Sam leaning against the door. "Pop, the building's in good shape. I went through it with the super."

"Good," said Simon. "You're starting to talk like an architect again."

"Not really. I just would like one of the apartments."

"You can't afford a furnished room!" laughed Simon.

"I thought we could work something out?"

"If I buy it, I'll see what I can do."

"Just until you tear it down," said Sam.

"I'm not so sure I want to tear it down. You'll have a long wait anyway. It's fully rented."

"No, it isn't," said Sam. "There's an empty apartment on the second floor."

Simon stopped what he was doing and turned towards his son. "An empty apartment?"

"They had trouble keeping it rented and just gave up."

"Is it haunted?" asked Simon casually as he turned his attention back to the egg in his hand.

"Then you heard the story?" said Sam.

"No, but you can bet it's all bull. I had a problem with a ghost in a building I owned on Madison Avenue. When the former owner renovated he pulled out part of an old waste stack. The wind rushing over the roof vent sounded just like a woman screaming."

"I told Bernie and the super it was something like that, but you know what they said?"

"What?" asked Simon.

"The old tenants not only heard noises.... they saw people walking through the walls."

"Bullshit!" said Simon.

"That's exactly what I said," answered Sam.

"Crap," thought Simon. "If Ray hears that he'll try to tell me that the C.I.A. is running a training camp in the dumbwaiter shaft."

# 17

Jimmy Callahan nursed a glass of wine in the Broadway Cafe opposite Memorial as he tried to start a conversation with two pretty, young Juilliard students lunching at a rear table. "You girls dancers?" he asked.

The girl that was doing all the talking nodded in reply, practically, but not quite, ignoring him at the same time. "Sorry," he said, "I should know when I'm not wanted." Callahan returned to the bar as the girl that had remained silent whispered to her friend, "I wouldn't have sent him away so fast. He's a gorgeous hunk of man."

"Just another stuck up actor," said the talkative girl. "And I wouldn't call him gorgeous. Rugged is more like it."

"That's just what I like," said the quiet girl. "Rugged!"

"Then why didn't you open your mouth?" asked her friend.

Callahan was about to order another wine when he saw the gray Ford wagon from the pickup service stop by the driveway next to the main entrance of Memorial. He put his glass down, told the bartender, "I'll take care of the tab later. This is the stiff I've been waiting for," and hurried across the street. He entered the funeral home by the front entrance, ignored Kaplan in the manager's office, turned right by the elevator, went into the garage and pressed the button to open the overhead door to allow the station wagon to back in. He went around to the rear gate of the wagon and asked the driver, "How's business?"

"This is it for the weekend," replied Callahan.

"He was murdered. A mugging or something," said the driver as he opened the back of the wagon and he and Callahan pulled the body bag out and placed it on a cart. "Geisler. I picked him up at the morgue."

"I hope they didn't do a full autopsy on him."

"Just his chest. Knife wounds." The driver held out a receipt pad and a ball point pen. Callahan said, "Give it to Kaplan in the office. I don't believe in signing anything." He pushed the cart into the service elevator and pressed the basement button.

He left the body in the embalming room while he took off his overcoat and jacket, hung them in the store room, and put on a rubber apron and his work shoes. Returning to the embalming room, he pushed the cart alongside of his work table, unzipped the body bag, and then rolled the corpse over onto the table top. Callahan then shoved the cart out of the way with his foot, picked up a plastic bottle of Fantastic, sprayed the corpse with it, and then rinsed it off with a hose.

When Kaplan came down into the basement, the pump was already going and Callahan was waiting to see how the skin tone would come up before applying make-up. Kaplan said, "Don't kill yourself. The casket will remain closed."

"I figured I'd fix him up a little, boss. You know, there's always someone who might want to take a look."

"As you say, who knows? They want as close to orthodox as possible, but they don't want a plain box and they don't want a shroud. A plain box! A shroud! No embalming! That's an orthodox funeral. These people want semi-orthodox. What's semi-orthodox?"

"Kaplan, this guy isn't Jewish."

"How do you know? He didn't tell you."

"Come on Kaplan, take a look. It's staring you in the face."

## 18

Ray left the hotel early, had breakfast at a coffee shop on West Fifty Second Street, and then walked up to Memorial. As he crossed Columbus Avenue, Gilda's Buick station wagon pulled up abreast of him. She rolled down the window and called out, "Ray, Simon went ahead to pick you and Morris up in his car."

Ray replied, "He didn't tell me he was coming. What's the whole family doing here?"

"Simon insisted. We'll see you after we park this monster."

Ray entered Memorial to be greeted by Pitchnik, as dour as ever, who asked, "Where is Mr. Blake? We have a distinct problem!"

"He's on the way. What's up?"

"Are you sure that Geisler was his uncle?"

"What's up?" Ray did not remember Pitchnik's name.

"Talk to the Rabbi. I'm extremely embarrassed." Pitchnik took a strong grip on Ray's arm and directed him into Kaplan's office.

As they entered, Rabbi Rose, a tall, baby faced redhead got up from a chair and said, "Mr. Blake?"

"No, Ray Warren. I'm an associate of his. What's up?"

"How well did you know Max Geisler?" asked the Rabbi.

"Never met him. What's up?"

Kaplan leaned back in his desk chair and said, "I think we'd better wait for Mr. Blake to explain things."

"Would you guys please tell me what's up?"

"We don't think that Max Geisler was Jewish."

"So what?" asked Ray. "The sign outside says nondenominational."

"The question is the Rabbi's officiating," said Kaplan. "The deceased may have preferred—"

"That's not the question at all," said the Rabbi. "The question is that the man you have in that coffin is not Max Geisler."

"It is Max Geisler! I knew him for years," said Pitchnik almost shouting.

"Did he ever tell you that he was Jewish?" asked the Rabbi.

"I assumed as much!" shouted Pitchnik. "You showed me him. I looked. It was the same Geisler that rented from me for years."

The Rabbi held up a copy of *The New York Times* and shouted back at Pitchnik, "Your Max Geisler is not David Moishe Geisler the son of a Rabbi."

As Ray took the newspaper from the Rabbi, he asked, "Rabbi, what brings this all up?"

"All Jews are circumcised. Mr. Blake's uncle isn't."

"Couldn't he be a convert?"

"Not the uncle of Simon Blake who has been noted for his generosity to many worthy causes including my temple which he never once set foot in."

When Ray finished reading the obituary he thought, Is this all? *It's just like some jerk in the agency to spend a fortune to plant someone in deep cover as a Jew and screwing up on an obvious point. But why somebody as easily identifiable as an actor? The body obviously isn't Geisler's. The man Simon described meeting wasn't as old as the obituary says.* Ray handed the newspaper back to the Rabbi and asked, "When did this guy come to the States?"

"Nineteen Forty Five," said Pitchnik. "He was naturalized in Fifty Three."

"Are you sure?"

"He was my tenant for thirty years."

Why? thought Ray. *They had all the war dead to pick from. Men without families. This is stupid.* Then Ray thought he had the answer. *The God damn Russians penetrated Binney's World War Two operation. They're the only ones who could have been so stupid. The guy they planted in Israel wasn't circumcised.*

He came up with a ruse to cool the matter down until he could contact the proper authorities. He said, "Geisler managed to hide out in Munich, say, six years. I assumed that he took another identity. He was an actor and could have pulled that off. He could have also found a friendly doctor, a plastic surgeon, and completed the disguise. I mean, Rabbi, I would have done a lot more under the same circumstances."

"I never heard of such an operation," said Kaplan.

"I've heard of others even more surprising," replied Ray.

"A devoted Jew wouldn't submit to such a procedure," said the Rabbi.

"Come, Geisler was an assimilated German," said Ray.

"That's what they all thought they were," said Kaplan.

"We're not discussing the Holocaust now," said the Rabbi. He asked Ray, "Are you a doctor?"

"No," said Ray, "but I've had experience in these matters. I was with the Central Intelligence Agency for thirty years and if you don't believe that, just look me up in *The New York Times* index."

Kaplan said, "I still never heard of such an operation."

"Mr. –" The Rabbi fumbled for Ray's name.

"Warren!"

"Mr. Warren, I think we should turn this matter over to the police. God knows who we are burying."

"I think you should wait for Simon Blake before taking action," said Ray strongly.

The Rabbi nodded. Ray dashed out of the office and through the front doors of the funeral home almost bowling over Sam and Gilda. He asked them quickly, "Simon?"

Gilda shrugged. Ray said, "I'll catch up with you later." He ran to the curb and looked for Simon's car, paced nervously for a moment and then ducked into a grocery store, bought a small bag of pretzels, and then returned to the street where he saw Simon and Morris approaching the funeral home on foot from the direction of Broadway. As he started towards them, he ripped open the bag and bit into one of the pretzels to calm himself down. He said, "Simon, I think you just hit it lucky."

"Hit it lucky?"

"An angle to snare the building. The guy in there isn't Max Geisler."

"I'll take a look," said Simon.

"He's not Max Geisler the comedian!"

"I met Max Geisler the building manager," said Simon calmly. "The comedian part came from my son. He never gets anything right."

After Ray filled him in on the details of his conversation at the funeral home, Simon said, "Don't think I'm going to stand still spending three grand to bury a Russian spy. Let's call the papers and blow this thing open."

"Shut up and have a pretzel." Ray handed the bag to Simon and then took Morris aside and said, "He doesn't understand. This has to be kept quiet until I contact the proper people in Washington."

"Bull!" said Simon.

Morris said softly, "Simon, let me handle this. We may be going off half-cocked. It may all be just a gross misunderstanding. I'll take a look at the body. Tell them I'm a doctor."

## 19

"He was a great artist then," said Rabbi Rose as he and Morris got off the elevator on the ground floor of the funeral home.

"More of a down to earth comedian," replied the sad looking lawyer.

"A German Jack Benny?" asked the young Rabbi.

"I wouldn't compare him to Jack Benny. Geisler was very broad, very Bavarian."

"I should have liked to have seen one of his films. Are there any available?"

"I doubt if they ever shipped a print of one over here. They weren't very exportable or memorable as motion pictures, even German ones."

As they turned into the main lobby, Simon rose from his seat besides Gilda and asked, "Is everything okay?"

The Rabbi nodded.

"Good .... okay," said Simon. "Rabbi, I'd like you to meet my family." As Simon introduced the Rabbi to Gilda, Sam, Charlene, Tina, and her husband, Art Norman, Morris casually drifted over to Ray and whispered, "I think we have to talk."

"What did you find out?" asked Ray.

The look in Morris's eyes said, *Not here!*

Ray nodded to show that he understood. Morris patted him on the back and then walked over to Simon and touched his shoulder. "I don't believe that the service will begin immediately. Ray and I are going to grab a quick cup of coffee."

Simon whispered to Morris, "Was he Crowell Collier?"

"No! We'll be across the street." Morris patted Simon on the back and hurried out the front door after Ray who said on the street, "I saw a coffee shop on the corner."

"I think this calls for a drink," said Morris.

"It's bad then?" asked Ray.

"Worse than that .... That place looks open." Morris indicated the Broadway Cafe and both men started across the street.

"The guy wasn't Geisler?" asked Ray.

"That's for damn sure," said Morris.

Simon came out of the funeral home behind them and shouted, "Hey you guys, wait up." He paused for a break in the traffic and then ran after them. "God damn it, I thought you were only going for coffee. It's not even noon. Morris, please don't get drunk until after the funeral. My family is here."

"I think you're the one that's going to get drunk," said Morris pulling the door of the restaurant open before him and then holding it open for Simon and Ray.

Simon snapped, "I don't drink this early. What did you tell the Rabbi?"

"There was extensive plastic surgery," said Morris looking over to the day bartender who was counting up the change in the cash register.

"Then it was Geisler?"

"No," said Morris sliding into one of the booths. "Sit down!" When Ray and Simon seated themselves, Morris asked softly, "Why that building?"

"I told you, I came across it by accident."

"I think you opened a can of worms."

"I don't understand," said Simon.

Ray nudged Simon with his elbow. "I think you stumbled into a bit of the old espionage game. A deep Russian plant."

"A what?" asked Simon. "Don't start jerking me off."

"The guy wasn't Russian," said Morris. "He was German. A former SS man. My guess, a Class B war criminal."

"Morris!" shouted Simon. "Don't tell me I'm spending three grand to bury a war criminal."

"That's my opinion," said Morris.

"It's not just an opinion if he had an SS tattoo on his arm!" shouted Simon.

Ray glanced at the bartender and motioned for Simon to remain silent. "Nobody's going to know. So keep it down."

"I'll know. Let the body rot on the street." Simon stood up. "I'm going to cancel the funeral."

"No!" said Ray as he reached up and pulled Simon back into the booth. He then asked Morris, "Does he really have an SS serial number?"

Simon began to mumble under his breath.

Ray raised a warning finger and said, "Look, buddy, just keep your cool for a minute."

Morris said, "No, he didn't have a tattoo. But there's an artful scar under the arm where one would have been. I've seen them before. I believe I took testimony from a Doctor in Aachen who was responsible for a number of similar such erasures."

"Jesus Christ!" Ray told Simon. "You've nabbed yourself a war criminal."

"Hold on!" replied Morris. "We don't have a Martin Borman. Any major Nazi would be in his eighties today. Our friend across the street wasn't much over sixty. I'm sixty five and I'm not in as good a shape as he is."

"Except for the fact that he's dead," said Ray. "Which means this is all just spitting in the wind."

Simon sputtered, "Spitting in the wind? I'm committing sacrilege burying the bum. A religious ceremony on top of everything. I have to tell the Rabbi."

"You're burying a dead body," said Ray. "The Rabbi is honoring Max Geisler, the real Max Geisler."

"I don't like the thought of that stiff resting in a Jewish cemetery."

Ray said, "He isn't going to rest there very long, buddy. I'm heading back down to D.C. tonight. I'll get this matter to the right people."

"Shit!" said Simon.

"You started it when you became obsessed with that lousy apartment building."

Simon scratched his nose and then asked, "Okay? Where's the real Geisler?"

Morris replied, "I don't think he was as successful in eluding the Gestapo as somebody would have us think."

"Hey, Morris," said Ray. "You've been around the cloak and dagger game. Why the hell would anybody switch identities with someone as easily recognizable as Geisler when any D.P. would have done the trick at the end of the war?"

"I haven't the slightest idea," replied Morris.

## 20

The stewardess with boney features and thin arms stopped in the aisle next to Ray and asked in a whisper, "Mr. Warren?"

"Yes," replied Ray looking up from a copy of "Lady Midas" by Jane Scott that Simon had given him.

"Ray Warren?" asked the stewardess with a touch of awe in her voice.

Ray nodded. The stewardess then pressed a piece of paper into his hand and said in a whisper, "From the Dulles tower."

"Thanks!" said Ray. He waited for the girl to continue on down the aisle before reading the note which said, "Mario Sculluzzi will pick you up at the arrival gate." Ray thought, *At least the guys at Langley are on the ball. Jesus, I hope this Geisler thing is big enough for me to get back on the inside with a little respect. That's all I want. Don't they know that?*

Mario Sculluzzi was a short rotund guy clad in a checkered sports coat and a cheap, wash and wear shirt without a tie. He didn't look the company type at all, too ethnic, but he was obviously the only American of Italian descent waiting at the arrival gate. They both nodded from a distance and then Sculluzzi rushed up with his hand extended and said, "Ray? Mario Sculluzzi."

Ray nodded carefully.

Sculluzzi continued, "I'll give you a lift. Let's get your luggage."

"I don't have any."

"Are you with the agency?" asked Ray as they headed out of the terminal.

"Immigration and Naturalization."

"I should have bet they'd pass the buck," said Ray. He thought, *Bastard! They're not taking me seriously.* He said to Sculluzzi, "I don't think this is your ball game."

"The hell it isn't. I'm a Nazi specialist."

"I didn't know they still had budgets for Nazi specialists."

"They don't. I'm retired," replied the jovial little man. "Tracking them down is my hobby."

*Shit,* thought Ray. *They're not taking this seriously!* He said sarcastically, "What do you do when you're not chasing Martin Borman?"

"He's dead," said Sculluzzi.

The two men walked on silently, Ray sure that he was up against a dead end.

Ray finally said, "I think you're the wrong guy for the job. If this stiff is anything he's a Russian plant."

"No!" said Sculluzzi. "I love the Russians. I hit Berlin on VE day plus three. They really gave the Krauts what they deserved. I still work with them. They didn't forget as fast as we did."

"No? This is more than just a low grade war criminal on the run. Who in his right mind would change identities with a well-known personality? A Jew on top of it all?"

"Someone did!"

"Why?"

"Because it was convenient. Because it took balls. I mean, if he tried to pass himself off as an ordinary D.P. people would think twice. Nobody would believe that anyone would have the nerve to pass himself off as Max Geisler. A little plastic surgery—"

"A lot of plastic surgery."

"Okay, a lot of plastic surgery. This guy figures he's about the same height and weight as Geisler and keeps him on the hook until he needs him and then tosses him into the ovens just as the good guys are approaching."

"That's only a theory," said Ray.

"A good one. I'll bet the stiff was a real stinker. He was too young to be a big shot, so he must have been out on the line doing the murdering and raping."

"You know it's all a load of shit," replied Ray. "Ancient history! Who really cares anymore? Your man's dead. You can't hang a corpse."

"If it's confirmed that your stiff is a wanted war criminal, I want to find out how he got over here. It'll lead us to more of those old bastards."

"That's it, old bastard!" said Ray. "If Geisler does lead you to anyone they'll be in a nursing home and that would be like shooting fish in a barrel."

# 21

Ray watched Sculluzzi drive off, and then, as he turned to enter the garden apartment complex in which he lived, his eyes drifted upwards and stopped on his own living room window. He noticed the reflection of a television screen in the right hand corner of one pane and fantasized a company hit team waiting in his flat. He told himself, *Stupid me! I stumbled into something big. What we used to call a stone best left unturned.*

He hurried up the single flight of stairs to his front door, his fantasy shattered by the fact that he might have left the set on went he left for New York. Then he recalled, *No, I didn't leave it on. I watched a God damn good British movie until four in the morning and I distinctly remember turning the thing off.*

Ray stopped in front of the door, listened to the sound of the set, and then rang the bell. There was no answer. Ray rang once more and then knocked loudly. There was still no answer.

He inserted his key into the lock and opened the door expecting a blast of cyanide or whatever such foolishness his former employers had in store for him. He told himself, *I suppose I'll have to put up some sort of fight and make a show of it.*

Ray stepped into living room with more curiosity than caution to be greeted by the sight of Cyrus Braddock slumped in an easy chair, shoeless, a can of beer in his hand, eyes glued to a busty brunette in a T-shirt cavorting on the television screen.

Cyrus Braddock! The eternal Special Assistant to the Director! The public relations voice of the Central Intelligence Agency. One of the few, old-line hacks who had sense to stay off an active desk and concentrate on glad handling politicians and the press. Cyrus Braddock! The aristocrat who constantly excused himself by stating, "Let's face it, you know and I know that I'm here on account of an impressive resume. No one has any real confidence in me, most of all myself."

Ray locked the door, crossed the room to Braddock, and whispered, "Has the shit hit the fan?"

Braddock waved Ray away with a small gesture that also meant hello, his eyes never turning from the brunette on the television's screen. He said, "Wait till this is over. I love big boobs .... Here I am on the far side of fifty, a latent dirty old man."

"Can I get a drink?"

"It's your apartment," said Braddock. When the brunette finally faded from the screen, he sighed, rose, went over to the kitchenette where Ray was freeing some ice from a tray, and said, "You're a bit late."

"I had a drink with that guy from immigration." Ray poured himself a stiff bourbon. "As I said, has the shit hit the fan? You wouldn't be here otherwise."

"You may have hit it big, friend."

"We'd better turn up the T.V. so we can talk."

"The place has been swept."

"Then it's really big? I hope I didn't open a can of worms."

"No, this is a goodie," said Braddock taking his old seat back.

"This guy, the one posing as a comedian, did us a big favor during the war and the OSS set him up with a new identity. Public relations, right? It could be embarrassing—"

"The comedian?" asked Braddock.

"The stiff Immigration and Naturalization is going to dig up tomorrow."

"Embarrassing? No. We're going to leak it to the press!"

"That we made a deal with the Nazis?"

"Yes!"

"That's not very good publicity," said Ray, skeptically.

"When I get through with it, it will be!"

"How?"

"The building."

Ray asked, "Then you know the whole story?"

"Know? I'm making up the whole story."

"A scam?"

Braddock nodded.

"Okay," said Ray. "Judge Foster Binney. Dropped into Bavaria in forty five, right? He was caught by the Gestapo, right? He manages to escape almost as fast, and you know better than anyone else that it doesn't happen like it happens in the movies. He didn't throttle a couple of guards and climb over the wall. The fix was in. Binney, being the man that he is, keeps his word and sneaks one of them out of Europe and into an apartment building on West Eighty-Third Street."

"Who did he sneak out?" asked Braddock.

"A big shot Nazi."

Braddock shook his head and then said, "Try again."

"Who else would they have to spirit out of Europe at the end of the war?"

"The owner of the building!"

"Crowell Collier?" gasped Ray.

Braddock nodded.

Ray said, "Crowell Collier? What does he have to do with the price of rice in China? No one is even sure he owned the building."

"Let's assume that that's an accepted fact."

"Okay, we have Crowell Collier," answered Ray. "What next?"

"What happened to him?"

"Let's not play What happened to Crowell Collier? Nobody will ever figure that out."

"That's why he's perfect for the stunt," said Braddock. "What do you think happened to him?"

"His mother murdered him."

"Good! You read one of the books. The one by Jane Scott. It's a hunk of junk. Armanda didn't murder Crowell. He was the only thing she had in life besides money."

"Okay!" said Ray. "Why did Crowell take a walk? She was a very domineering lady. She kept him under her thumb. She didn't want to spoil him. The books says she never gave him a nickel. A small allowance."

"A small allowance?" asked Braddock.

"Two hundred dollars a week!"

"That wasn't what you would call small in Nineteen Ought Five."

Ray thought for a moment and then said, "He ran off with a broad!"

"No one, my friend, except in grand opera, walks away from a hundred million dollars for a broad. Not any of the broads I've been fortunate enough to meet."

"I take it you now have the facts suitably re-arranged?"

Braddock nodded.

Ray said, "Okay! Crowell was a Captain in World War One. National Guard. Bought his commission."

"That was in the book. But Jane Scott never mentioned that he went to Russia in Nineteen Eighteen while still in uniform."

"Is that a new fact or an old one?"

"An old one. And, another old one is that he went as an intelligence officer."

"Now I read you," said Ray. "He was one of us!"

Braddock smiled. "Armanda wanted to make something out of him. He didn't do too well at Yale. She packed him off to Heidelberg."

"Okay! Old fact! He spoke fluent German."

"In nineteen fifteen he went to Berlin. Old fact."

"New fact! Ostensibly looking after momma's business, but he's actually a high ranking intelligence operative."

"New fact! After World War One he planted himself in Germany for good."

"Okay," said Ray, "Suppose you have Crowell Collier as the original Allen Dulles. I don't get the scam. We didn't have an effective intelligence gathering organization back then. And, from what I heard, Crowell had a hard time lacing his shoes in the morning. Not your typical super spy."

"What if that was an act? What if he didn't work for an official branch of the government? What if he was supported by people like Armanda? The Rockerfellers? The Duponts? They were quite concerned with the rise of Communism."

"New fact! Crowell Collier walked out of one day in Nineteen Twenty Four to partake in a clandestine operation in the service of big business and was killed in the line of duty. New Fact! The mission was so sensitive that his death had to remain a mystery. What does that have to do with a dead SS man passing himself off as a Hebe comedian sixty six years later?"

"New fact. Crowell didn't die on that mission!"

"New fact. He was planted someplace in Europe to subvert Communism! Hey, Braddock, guys who plan to inherit millions don't do that sort of stuff."

"New fact! He thought it was only for a short time, but when he saw how things were developing in Europe he decided to remain as an agent in place. New Fact. Crowell Collier was up there in the Nazi hierarchy!"

"What did he contribute?" asked Ray. "Ninety percent of our intelligence came from Ultra, not an agent in place."

"What if he worked in another way? What if he fouled up the Germans on a policy making level? What if he was the guy that convinced Hitler to invade Russia?"

"Who controlled him?"

"Judge Foster Binney. He made numerous trips to Germany between Nineteen Twenty Five and Nineteen Thirty Eight. In forty five, they pulled the Colonel out of a line outfit and dropped him into Germany. For what? I'll tell you what! To get Crowell out!"

"Why didn't Crowell turn face up after the war?"

"Would you if you were operating as a Nazi?" said Braddock.

"Do you have anything to back this all up?"

"Not yet. It's bullshit," said Braddock. "But suppose someone in the United States, officially or unofficially, was smart enough to sprinkle a half dozen Crowell Colliers throughout the world between Nineteen Twenty and Nineteen Forty one. Better than Ultra, right?"

"Sure, but where are they now that we need them?"

"Created and postdated following us going public with what 'really' happened to Crowell Collier. The media will eat it up and the Goddamn Reds will take it as Gospel truth."

"Shit, we could work back from each and every one of their major disasters, even the economic ones, and attribute them to one of our plants. We use some of their guys with fuzzy backgrounds that are safely dead and buried. Braddock, you're a genius."

"I know! It'll wreak havoc with the Communist Block's long term planning. They'll waste millions of man hours checking out everybody in a key position older than fifty."

"After we do our homework, we'll leak the Crowell Collier story to a solid, liberal journalist. Let him be the motivating force. Let him dig up the planted facts. Let him win the Pulitzer Prize."

"Then we see eye to eye," said Braddock. "Officially you still have nothing to do with the agency, but you're back on the payroll. You'll report only to me."

"A couple of questions?"

"Shoot!"

"The weak links. What if Crowell Collier turns up again?"

"The odds are against it. He would be over ninety."

"Binney?"

"He's not in on it."

"When it gets in the papers?"

"He'll deny it, but who's going to believe him. He was once one of us."

## 22

Simon felt a little bit silly drinking cheap wine out of a paper cup in Bernie Global's apartment in the building cluttered with camera equipment and thrift shop furniture, but he had to admire Morris who was seated next to Sam on a tattered couch. The old lawyer seemed totally at ease with the kids in the room.

The conversation had centered around Max Geisler for a good half hour but Simon was more concerned with his son's girlfriend. It was obvious that Sam had been going with her for some time although he never divulged the fact to his family. The girl was Irish, rather bland looking, on the heavy side, and also a "film-maker."

Bernie's wife, a dark, intense girl drew Simon back to the subject at hand by stating, "He was one of the sweetest men I ever met. I was a shame what happened to him. That's what you get when you live in New York."

"Happened to who?" asked Simon.

"Max Geisler," said Bernie refilling Simon's paper cup. "A nice guy. Real Old World charm."

Simon looked at Morris out of the corner of his eye and said to himself, *Nice guy, my ass.*

Bernie's wife said, "He had a beautiful voice. He used to sing for us. We invited him to all our parties."

"Yeah," said Bernie. "He was okay. There are people in this building who went three and four months without paying the rent and he carried them."

"Including us," said the wife.

Simon got up, put his paper cup on the radiator, and said, "I'd like to take a look at that empty apartment now."

"Sure," said Bernie. "I'll show it to you."

Simon turned to Sam and asked, "Sam?"

"I saw it already."

Simon shrugged and followed Bernie out into the hall. Bernie said, "There's nothing interesting about it. It's just an empty, two bedroom apartment. Let's take the stairs. The elevator sucks."

As he unlocked the door of the upstairs apartment, Bernie added, "I use it for shooting once in a while."

Entering, Simon asked, "Where are the ghosts?"

"If there are any, I never saw one," said Bernie turning on the lights.

Simon gave the living room a quick once over, took a quick look in the bedrooms, opened a couple of closet doors, and then muttered, "Nothing special."

"What did you expect to find?"

"Nothing! It's just an old, run of the mill West side apartment. And, as usual, some idiot painted over what must have been twenty thousand dollars of custom wood work." Simon opened the door to a bathroom, took a quick look inside, and said, "You don't see fixtures like that anymore."

Back in his apartment, Bernie asked, "How about everybody hanging in for dinner? I'll whip something up."

"Not me," said Simon, "But Morris will take you all out for steaks."

"Me?" said Morris.

"Charge it to the company."

Sam asked, "Aren't you coming along, Pop?"

"I have a date!"

"Business?" asked Morris.

"Business but none of your business," laughed Simon.

## 23

Morris finished the wine in his cup thinking that Simon was playing it too cute, disgustingly cute. *The bastard is on to me! Why doesn't he come out and say it. Why is he torturing me? Why did he wait for so many years?*

## 24

Simon parked the Seville in an empty space by a meter on 89th Street and 2nd Avenue, gazed at a slip of paper in his hand, and then crossed the street to Elaine's wondering why Jane Scott hadn't chosen a more convenient part of the city to meet in. Opening the restaurant's door, he gave the front room a quick look over, ignored a voice that asked him if he wanted a table, went to the back room, glanced around, and then returned to the bar where he ordered a glass of white wine. Checking his wrist watch he thought, *that was what you could expect from a writer.*

When his wine came, Simon stopped eyeing the door expectantly and began to study the other patrons in the place. A petite blonde, about his daughter's age, dressed in a jeans suit and turtle neck sweater seemed to be studying him intensely.

Oh, my, a hooker joint, he thought. He took a sip of wine and looked towards the door not failing to notice the blonde again.

She smiled.

Simon felt extremely embarrassed. He jerked his head away and he had to do all he could to keep from blushing.

He looked at the girl again out of the side of his eye and thought, Oh, my God, she's coming over here.

She walked directly up to him and asked, behind his hunched back, "Are you Simon Blake?"

Simon turned and said, "Yeah!"

The girl replied, "I'm Jane Scott."

The pressure came off so quickly that Simon burst into laughter as he turned to face her. "You've got to be kidding. I have kids older than you. You wrote a whole book?"

"Right! That's me! The one and only."

"You were the only J. Scott in the telephone book."

"I am also the only one that wrote Lady Midas."

"I'm sorry," said Simon. "I expected somebody entirely different."

"So did I. I looked up your picture in the *Times* morgue this afternoon."

"Let's have dinner."

"That's what we're here for."

As Simon followed Jane back to her table, she said, "You don't look like your picture."

"You don't look like a writer. So what else is new?" Simon held out a chair for her.

As she sat, she said, "What did you expect, a little old lady in tweeds?"

"Is that what women writers look like?"

"What do men realtors look like? I thought you'd be fat. You look awful jowly in your pictures. You're actually handsome in a fatherly way. The touch of gray in your hair? Is it for real?"

"Only my hair dresser knows." He turned to a waiter and ordered another round of drinks. Then he said, "I'd better get some new publicity pictures. I lost weight since then."

"My editor was worried about my book jacket picture. He said that no one would take me seriously. He thought it made me look like a prep school girl."

"You do!" said Simon.

"Still?"

"Right!"

"The book was written eight years ago. I'm past thirty."

"That's still a teenager as far as I'm concerned," said Simon. "How come?"

"How come what?"

"Why did you write that book?"

"It started out as a thesis, but my professor was impressed enough to pass it on to a publishing house. Being a child prodigy hasn't paid off, Mr. Blake. I haven't sold another book yet and there weren't enough people interested in Armanda Collier to make me rich from the first one."

"Why did you pick Crowell to write about?"

"The book isn't about Crowell, it's about Armanda ....
She's from my hometown, Ambrose. It made the research easier."

## 25

Much later, halfway through dinner, Jane Scott looked up from her shrimp scampi and said to Simon, "That's it. You know all about me. Good, solid Wasp family, Vassar, rah, rah, rah, and all the right connections. The only thing you haven't asked is if I'm married or not."

"I know you're not married. You're not wearing a ring and you're here." Simon was amused by his reaction to Jane. He had barely touched his food and knew he was a big enough fool to start worrying about his weight just because he was sitting with a pretty, young girl. "Now that the small talk is over, tell me who owns that building?"

"The whole answer is going to cost you money."

"I wouldn't think of it not costing me money. I found out a long time ago that anything I've ever gotten for free turned out to be extremely expensive in the long run."

"Like the first time you made it with your wife."

"Nope! She has always been an asset. I would be a poor man today if I didn't get married as soon as I got out of the army. I needed the responsibility."

"I bet you and your wife didn't even have sex until the honeymoon."

"That was how it was done in the old days. Let's get back to the building. I would be happy to pay you any reasonable amount for your time."

"Six million dollars?" asked Jane without cracking a smile.

"The building isn't worth that much,"

"I want to put you into the movie business. I want you to invest six million dollars in the movie version of my book."

"No!" said Simon. "I wouldn't touch show business with a ten foot pole."

"Robert Redford would be perfect for Crowell Collier. He's reading the script now."

"Robert Redford doesn't impress me, kid, and I can't stand anybody in show business. I haven't gone to a movie in years."

"But you read?"

"When I'm forced to."

"Lady Midas can make a lot of money for you."

"Count me out," said Simon. "But I'll tell you what I will do for you. I'll introduce you to some people in that racket that may be interested. I have a lot better things to do with six million dollars."

"Okay," said Jane. "But remember, I'll make you keep your word .... Judge Foster Binney owns the building."

"No! That avenue has been explored."

"He won't sell because he ripped it off from Armanda. The title isn't clear."

"He isn't the type that jiggles people," said Simon.

"Jiggle? He was Crowell's best friend, more like a brother. He not only knew that Crowell was ripping his mother off, he had to be the brains behind the whole thing. He was in the perfect position to grab everything when Crowell disappeared. The real mystery is why he stopped with only the building."

"Binney's honest," said Simon.

"Crowell couldn't have taken his mother for a nickel. He was dim witted, an alcoholic, and a hedonist."

"He became a Captain in the army."

"National Guard! He was the most incompetent officer in the A.E.F. He spent more time in Paris than in the trenches."

"This all comes from your research?" asked Simon.

"Direct from the lips of my grandfather, his executive officer."

"I'd like to talk to your grandfather," said Simon.

"He isn't with us anymore but I have him on tape."

"Okay," replied Simon. "I'll buy the fact that Crowell was a bum, but I won't buy the story that his mother murdered him."

"Neither do I," said Jane.

"But that was what your book said!"

"Armanda wouldn't have had him murdered. He was all she had in the world."

"You're telling me you lied in print?"

Jane nodded. "I had to. My publisher said we had to have a commercial hook. Something they could base the advertising and promotion on. I mean, some people said they thought she did him in, but they didn't do the research that I did and they weren't from her home town like I am."

"Fucking around with history is worse than murder."

"Shoot me."

"Okay," said Simon. "What happened to him?"

"Ask anyone around Ambrose. Crowell flipped his lid and the old lady stashed him in an institution. Some say it was syphilis. Who knows? In any case, it wasn't as exciting as having him murdered by his mother."

"What else do you have on him that isn't in the book?"

"Tons of material. You know, that story is true."

"What story?"

"Binney's from Ambrose. One of an immigrant mill worker's twelve kids. Armanda found him foraging through a garbage can one day and said to her driver, "Let's take him home and fatten him up." She took a liking to Foster, gave his old man a couple of bucks, and raised him like her own. Put him through Yale and Harvard Law. She said, 'Just to get my investment back. God damn lawyers charge a fortune these days'."

Simon said, "And he ended up ripping her off?"

"You would have, too. She didn't endear herself to the people closest to her. I mean, she treated Binney better than her son."

"I'd like to see your research material."

"I'd like to you to read my movie script."

"Okay!" said Simon. "It's a deal, but you won't get a nickel out of me."

At they left the restaurant, Simon decided that Jane Scott was damn cute even though she had a pug nose. He said, "I'll drive you home."

"And pick up the script!"

Simon nodded. Jane took his hand and led him towards the corner. "We can walk. I'm between First and York."

"We'll take the car," said Simon feeling a bit silly. He hadn't held hands with a girl since he dated his wife.

## 26

Jane held the door open for Simon. He entered her apartment, stopped, and studied the single, studio room before looking out the window. "Say, a little terrace. Did the shutters come with the place?"

"My father put them in." Jane went to the fireplace, took an artificial log from a copper scuttle, placed it on the hearth, and lit it.

"Not bad at all," said Simon still looking around. "Whoever renovated this brownstone did it with class. Most New York City landlords are bums."

"Ours is okay," replied Jane. "I still would like a bedroom."

"You don't need any more space." Simon sat on a director's chair opposite the convertible couch. "I wish I had a place like this. I envy you."

Jane, bored with his chatter about her apartment, turned sharply and exited into the small kitchen. She said, "Is scotch okay? I don't have any wine."

"What's wrong?" asked Simon. "You sound angry."

"You're making fun of me."

"Me?"

Jane said, "I'm sure you have a neat little duplex on Park or Sutton with Harvey Probber furniture and a Jap house boy."

"I have a comfortable suburban home!" answered Simon. He didn't understand her at all.

"Expensive, I'm sure."

"No, not at all. Not by a long shot. It's part of a parcel I subdivided years ago. It's not a mansion if that's what you're thinking."

"You must have a bachelor pad?"

"I've never had a bachelor pad," said Simon. "I've never lived alone."

"Even in college?" said Jane running a tray under hot water to free up the ice.

"I didn't go to college. I was married when I returned home from the war. We lived with her parents until I bought a place under the G.I. Bill."

Jane went to a desk by the window. She picked up a bound manuscript, and placed it before him. She said, "Lady Midas, starring Robert Redford."

"And Barbra Streisand!"

"I don't think she'll make a convincing Armanda Collier."

"I'm too tired to read it now," said Simon.

"I wouldn't want you to read it in front of me. That would make me very nervous." Jane then said, "Why don't you take your coat off and relax?"

"Okay!" said Simon. "But I can't stay long. It's a long drive." He stood, took off his overcoat, and draped it over the back of a chair.

Jane said, "You can take your jacket off, too. It's hot in here. I'll put some music on. Anything in particular?"

"I'd rather not have music. I'm not every good at relaxing. I'd like to see the stuff you have on Crowell."

"Let's listen to some music," replied Jane as she dropped the tone arm on a record and the first strains of Aquarius filled the room.

"That's from Hair. I saw it. My wife had theater party tickets. I guess it dates me."

"It dates me, too," sighed Jane. "I saw the original production. I'm a wilted flower child."

"The stuff on Crowell?"

"It's all packed away at my parents."

"Get it down here! I'll set you up with an office. I'll put you on the payroll. Five hundred bucks a week. I want that building."

"I don't want your five hundred dollars a week," said Jane. "There's nothing left to research. Just relax. Can't you carry on a normal conversation? I find you very interesting."

"Just a warning, young lady. No matter what you offer me tonight, you're not going to jiggle six million dollars for a movie," laughed Simon.

"You have a lot more going for you than money," said Jane.

"You're making me very uncomfortable," said Simon.

"I happen to prefer older men," said Jane.

"I'd better go," said Simon quickly. "I didn't come up here to take advantage of you."

Jane laughed. "Take advantage of me?"

"Good night!" Simon picked up his overcoat, took the script, kissed Jane on the forehead, and went out the front door. He thought, *They all have their little scams, even writers.* When he got back to his car he sat and thought, *You were shaking in your boots, old man. What can you lose? How many more opportunities like this are you going to get?*

He drove to the telephone booth on the corner and dialed Jane's number. When she answered, he said, "I'm coming back up."

Jane was probably going to tell him no, but he hung up before she could reply. She was waiting on the landing as he came up the stairs. He hurried past her and sat down by the fire stating, "I want to stay the night."

"You sure have a lot of confidence."

"Not in these situations. This is a first time for me."

"A first time?"

"I never cheated on my wife. I've had opportunities but I always chickened out. There was never another woman. A couple of whores overseas, but that was a long time ago."

"Do you still love her?" asked Jane as she helped him off with his jacket.

"In a way, but I barely talk to her anymore. We live in two different worlds. She hasn't grown with me."

Jane put her finger to his lips and then her arms around his neck. After they kissed, Simon said, "I'm very nervous. Excuse me if nothing happens."

Jane whispered, "Anything you want will happen ....
Are you kinky?"

"Huh?" asked Simon.

"Do you want me to undress you?"

"I'd think I'd better have another drink," said Simon.

"You won't need one," replied Jane. You know what?
..... I think I will undress you." As she began to remove
Simon's tie, he blushed. Jane said, "I finally have you
figured out. You're nothing but a big baby."

## 27

*Yes*, thought the Judge. *There would be nothing at all wrong
in me paying my respects. They wouldn't care.* The Judge took his
pocket watch out and glanced at the back. There was a
serial number engraved on the case which he couldn't see
without the aid of his magnifying glass. Its last seven digits
was a telephone number that he had never dialed. He
doubted that it was still functioning. He doubted that
"they" still existed. *Still*, he thought, *They were younger men.
Younger than I. But .... not after all these years. There must have
been a recall. They must have been ordered to stand down.*

The Judge had Parri cancel all his appointments and
drive him out to Beth Shalom so he could say farewell to
Max Geisler Number Three. "He's was a friend, Parri. And
old one, a circumstantial one, but still a friend. I don't have
many left."

When they arrived at the cemetery, Parri went into the
office to ask the location of the grave. When he returned to
the car he said, "He isn't here anymore."

"What do you mean?" asked the Judge.

"His body has been moved."

The Judge took a moment to reply. He expected a shortness of breath, a rush of blood to his head, a stroke. Something to enable him to avoid having to deal with the problem at hand. He thought, *These aren't coincidences anymore. Simon Blake's interest in the building. Geisler's murder. The expropriation of the corpse. Of course! That's it! Control is still functioning.* He told Parri, "I think I would like to go to the office today. There's still time to do some work."

As they drove off the ramp of the West side Highway at West 58th Street, Binney said, "Cut across Fifty-fourth and drop me off at the first pay telephone. Come back in ten minutes!"

"It's not a safe neighborhood, Sir."

"Ten minutes!" snapped the Judge.

Judge Binney watched Parri drive off, went to the telephone, and took out his pocket watch. Using his pocket magnifier he read the last seven digits on the serial number of his watch case, dialing them at the same time. After three short rings a voice answered, "Control."

Binnie replied, "Control, this is Decoy."

"I recognize your voice, Decoy."

"Are you still operational?"

"We answered the phone didn't we, sir?" replied the pleasant voice on the other end of the wire.

Binney asked cautiously, "Simon Blake? Is he with you?"

"Negative," replied the voice.

"Control, listen carefully. The disposition of Max Geisler Number Three's body. Did you handle that?"

"We handled the disposition of Max Geisler Number Three. The operative left the body. There were no instructions in the procedure book about disposing of the body."

"Oh, my God," screeched the Judge. "Why?"

"He was in direct violation of orders. He tried to contact Max Geisler Number Two directly."

Binney shouted, "Don't you know it's all over! It's just a farce! Control, you're not to take any more actions. Understand?"

"I'm only going by standing orders, sir."

"You've murdered a poor, innocent, harmless old man."

"He tried to make direct telephone contact with Max Geisler Number Two."

"Telephone contact? I've visited him several times. You didn't murder me."

The voice replied, "We're understaffed due to normal attrition. We are only able maintain twenty four hour wire surveillance of the subject. Decoy, we would appreciate some young blood out here. All of us are way past retirement age. Put in a word for us, please."

"Put in a word with who, you idiot?" shouted the Judge. "Control, how many of you are left?"

"I can't divulge that, sir."

"God damn you! Where are you located? I have to talk to you in person."

"That's against standing orders!" answered the voice.

"Then listen to me carefully! This is a recall! This is a recall!"

"Please give me the prefix for recall, sir?"

"I don't know the prefix," said Binney.

"It's in your code book, sir," said the voice.

"They never gave me a code book."

"Then you aren't authorized to order recall, sir."

"They're all dead. There's nobody left alive that can order recall."

"Sir, we can't initiate a recall without the proper prefix," replied the voice politely.

Binney said, "Is there a procedure for terminating Max Geisler Number Two and disposing of the body?"

"Yes, sir!"

"Can you initiate that?"

"Yes, sir!"

"Then go ahead!"

"I would have to have the proper prefix for that too, sir."

"Please, Control, I beg you. Listen! There's no one left with a code book other than yourself."

"In that case, sir, would you please see about having them issue you a code book?"

Binney screamed, "Don't you understand? There are no more *thems*! I'm the last one left alive and they didn't issue me a code book."

"Thank you for calling, Decoy. I have to keep this line free. It's the only one, you know."

Binney slammed down the phone. For the first time in his life he felt his age. He began to blame everything on Simon Blake.

## 28

Somewhere along the line, someone in the chain of command decided that Judge Binney, who had already lost two sons in the war and whose life was an open book, required a security check. When it was felt that he could be trusted, they detached him to Oakridge, Tennessee, for orientation in atomic energy. The great secret he learned was they would soon be able to power a tank as long as a year with a single "magnetic fuel rod."

On his return to Washington he met Donavan away from the clutter of the official OSS office in the conference room of a firm of Attorneys on Constitution Avenue. Binney greeted Bill with a nod, lit a cigar, and said, "They tried to make a physicist out of me down there, but I couldn't understand half the jabberwocky they threw at me."

"But you understand that the substance we're sending you after is needed desperately."

"I don't see why. The war's almost over and I'm missing the best part of it."

"I'm sorry, but you're the only man for this assignment. We considered a lot of others, but you're the only one with enough maturity and brains to pull it off."

"That's bullshit! Any kid fluent in German could take a shot at it," said Binney. "No one on the Allied side ever considered me for this mission. I was asked for by name in Germany. Someone who finally saw the light of day and wanted to make a business arrangement with somebody they trust. A somebody that I know."

Donavan tried to change the subject. "Foster, the little adventure isn't as risky as you may think."

"Then you should have started sooner so I could have gotten to Munich in time for Fasching."

"I'm glad you haven't lost your sense of humor."

"I certainly haven't!" snapped Binney. "But don't take me for a fool! How much are you paying that woman?"

Donavan stood, paced for a moment, and then said, "You're way ahead of us."

"I have a habit of thinking things out. I didn't get to where I am today by my good looks. It's dear old Lily, isn't it? Hell, she's the only person I know in Germany."

"You just answered you own question."

"How much?"

"One million dollars cash which you are delivering to her."

Binney took a long puff on his cigar. "Well .... Even she knows that I won't disappear with the money between here and the drop zone. Who's she working for? Whoever it is, you just gave me the first God damn good reason to feel sorry for Nazi Germany."

"We don't know! But the information she's been supplying us with has been as good as gold."

"Knowing her she's probably been to bed with half the big shots in the Nazi party including Hitler himself. Then again..."

"Then what?" asked Donavan.

"She's no spring chicken. I assume you made a deal with her on war crimes?"

"War crimes?"

"She a naturalized American citizen."

"War crimes? What, screwing the right people?"

"I could find precedent. How am I going to get those magnetic fuel rods out Germany after I hand her the cash?"

"It's taken care of. Just confirm that she has access to them and then signal us."

"She'll hand me over to the dogs once she gets her hands on the money. You don't know her as well as I do."

"Not with Germany on the verge of collapse."

"Will I have a radio operator?"

"We have one in place in Munich."

"How do I get back to our lines after this little caper?" asked Binney.

"You don't," said Donavan. "You're going to have an open line to General Eisenhower. You're going to resolve the question of if, when, where, and how Hitler plans to make a last stand in the Alpenfestung, and you're going to contact an underground group in Munich, the Bavarian Action Party, and see what trouble you can stir up."

"Now that sounds like a job of work," said Binney. "I was beginning to think that I would be nothing but a messenger boy for a whore."

## 29

Ray suggested a Georgetown Pub for his second meeting with Sculluzzi, the Nazi specialist from Immigration. It was noisy, crowded, and no one would pay particular attention to the two men although they stood out among the regulars, mostly younger men. Ray waited with beer in hand at a tiny, corner table. Sculluzi, wearing the same outfit he had on at the airport bullied his way through the crowd at the bar and then slid into a seat.

"What are you drinking?" asked Ray.

"A beer's okay," said Sculluzzi sighing with exhaustion.

"Gotcha," said Ray as he rose and made his way to the crowded bar where he ordered a pitcher of beer. Returning with it to the table, he placed a glass in front of Sculluzzi and poured. "The service here is terrible. College kids."

Sculluzzi looked at the fresh glass of beer in front of him and then took a healthy swig. "Salute!"

Ray raised his glass in toast. "To Max Geisler."

"The stiff wasn't a war criminal," replied Sculluzzi as he wiped the foam from his lips with the back of his hand.

"No?"

"Absolutely!" said Sculluzzi.

"He was an SS man?"

Sculluzi nodded. "Yeah, but not what you would call a war criminal. He was a tenor."

"A tenor like in singer?" asked Ray not quite comprehending.

"A pretty boy named Rolph Liebhomm."

"But SS?"

"Yeah," replied Sculluzzi. "Honorary. Allgemeine! He was active with an entertainment and propaganda unit."

Ray refilled his glass from the pitcher. "One kraut is as good as another. Do you want to order a hamburger here or would you like to go some other place for dinner?"

"I'm not hungry," said Sculluzzi. "This Rolph Liebhomm guy? What was his gimmick?"

"You're asking me?" said Ray.

"I'm asking your opinion. We have a successful actor, a pretty boy, who did nothing for the Nazis other than sing songs running for his life in Forty five. Taking another man's identity. Why? Nobody was chasing him. He wasn't on any body's list."

"I'm going to order a hamburger," said Ray. He then said to Sculluzzi, "He panicked!"

"Why? He never saw combat and he never got within ten miles of a concentration camp."

"He had a guilty conscience. Some Germans had them, you know."

Sculluzzi shrugged, "I was told to leave it in your hands. That you may want to break the story to the press."

"How? We have a mystery wrapped around a mystery?"

"What?"

"Did you say you wanted to eat?" asked Ray.

# 30

Simon didn't realize how silly he had begun to act after he spent the night with Jane Scott. Instead of going to the office in the morning, he went to Tiffany's, bought her an expensive watch, and then hurried back up to her apartment with it. He said, "Just want to show my appreciation."

Jane looked at the slender package and said, "If it's something dreadfully expensive, I don't want it. I don't take costly gifts from men."

"It's just a little watch. Nothing pretentious," replied Simon.

"No way!" said Jane handing the package back to him. "I'm not against gifts, but it's too early in our relationship for me to accept them. When we get to know each other better."

"I want to do something for you," said Simon with tensed lips.

"Help me get my movie off the ground."

When Simon returned to his car, he decided what to do with the watch. Recalling Jane's words, "When we get to know each other better," he drove to his bank and asked for his safe deposit box. Not the one that contained the deed to his house, his insurance policies, and other things that his family would have easy access to, but the box that contained his personal mementos.

Secluded in a curtained alcove in the bank's basement, he opened the box and, instead of placing the watch inside immediately, went through the contents until he found a faded snapshot of himself, Ray, and Morris standing in front of his brand new M-4 tank on the Marienplazt in Munich a few days after the war ended. Simon couldn't believe how young they all looked in the photograph. Younger than even his son Sam. He then reached into the safe deposit box and removed an object neatly packaged in oiled, brown wrapping paper and tied with string. Simon unwrapped it to reveal a Luger automatic pistol with two clips of ammunition. It was the same Luger he had taken off the SS officer he had shot in Steinhoffen. He put it and the ammunition in his brief case.

When he returned to his office he decided to approach the acquisition of the building in a direct manner and not rely on Ray. He told his secretary, "I'd like to take an ad in *The New York Times*, the *Wall Street Journal*, the real estate trades, and all German language newspapers. Run it for a couple of weeks." Simon cleared his throat and then dictated, "Stockholders in the Three Eighty Nine West Eighty Third Street Corporation please write or telephone the undersigned as it will be to your benefit."

Simon's girl, Cathy, asked, "Is that all, Mr. Blake?"

"Yeah," he replied. He then called her back and added, "Place it in a couple of papers in West Germany and Israel, too. Especially Munich."

Ray telephoned a few minutes later and said, "I've come up with some interesting material on the building."

"Good! Hey, you know what I dug up today. The Luger I got in Steinhoffen. I got it with me. I thought you'd want to take a look at it again."

"If you insist, but I have two my own rusting away someplace. Simon, listen, I think I'm on to something. Crowell Collier owned that building after all."

Simon listened for a while and then said, "A super spy, huh? .... That's pretty jazzy. I'd like you to meet a young lady friend of mine. She wants to make a movie about Crowell and your story is much better than hers."

"Do you have a copy of the script?" asked Ray intrigued by the idea.

"Since when were you interested in movies?" asked Simon.

"I'm interested in Crowell Collier," said Ray.

"The script will be waiting for you at the office. It's by Jane Scott, the kid that wrote the book about his mother."

## 31

After the introductions, Jane Scott asked Ray, "Are you from Hollywood?"

"No," said Ray. "Where did you get that idea?"

"Simon!"

"He has a strange sense of humor. No, I'm a Washington lawyer."

"Then why the show business treatment?" asked Jane. "Lunch here at Sardi's?"

"That's what Simon suggested. I'm not much on New York restaurants."

Jane asked, "Simon said you'd like to make a movie from my script."

"No," replied Ray. "He should have said I know some people who are interested in the project. I passed the script along to them."

"It would be an expensive movie. You know, lots of old cars, costumes. You would have to practically rebuild my hometown. The old mills are all gone now."

"Six and a half million dollars!" said Ray. "They ran a budget up on it."

Jane looked directly into Ray's eyes. "You know, I'm beginning to think that you're serious."

"I loved your script," said Ray with a straight face.

"I have an agent," replied Jane quickly. "I mean, I'm not free to discuss money without her."

"She'll be contacted," said Ray.

"Have you ever produced a movie before?" asked Jane.

"I'm not producing the movie. A guy name Lloyd Bannerman is."

"Lloyd Bannerman. *The* Lloyd Bannerman? I don't believe you. There must be a catch."

"Well, the script needs work."

"I thought so," said Jane as if she had been just kicked in the stomach. "How much work?"

"Bannerman wants a different slant on the story."

"The most dramatic ending is to have Armanda kill Crowell and then go into seclusion wracked with remorse."

"They don't want an Armanda Collier story," said Ray slowly so that she was sure to understand.

"My book and script are about Armanda."

"They want a Crowell Collier story."

"Crowell? There wasn't much to Crowell. The only thing that he ever did noteworthy was to disappear."

"That's where I beg to differ. It'll be a war story."

"A war story?" Jane covered her face with her hands. Ray couldn't tell if she was laughing or crying. "A war story," she continued. "I didn't write a war story. I wrote about a business woman. Everyone knows that Crowell's contributions to the A.E.F. were minimal, if not negative."

"Actually," said Ray. "There's some material in a file down in Washington that I have access to that indicates Crowell may have been doing intelligence work on the sly."

"What kind of information? I put two full years in on the family and never came up with anything like that."

"That was before the Freedom of Information Act. I think I can lead you to a lot of material on Crowell that used to be classified."

Ray sold it well even though the movie wasn't his idea. When Braddock heard about the girl's script he took the ball and ran thinking that there would be no better way to sell Crowell as a hero than the medium of film. Jane Scott would be convinced that she, and she alone, was the one that uncovered Crowell's hidden life, his missing years, and his clandestine adventures.

"You people are crazy," said Jane. "I don't think I could write an espionage story even if I tried."

"Then you're not interested?"

"Of course I'm interested!"

## 32

"Looking for your relatives after all these years," said Mrs. Rosenthal as she refilled Ray's coffee cup in the 11th floor apartment of the building. "I'm sorry I can't be of more help."

"They're not my relatives," said Ray. "I'm an attorney. I'm trying to clear up an estate matter. The last known address for the Ritter family is here." Ritter was an X-factor name that he had pulled out of thin air.

"I know, you told me all that before. You'll have to excuse me. I'm not a young woman. My memory isn't too good. I can't really help you. It was nice of you to stay for coffee. I don't have many visitors these days. Mr. Geisler could have helped you, poor man." Mrs. Rosenthal pushed a plate of cookies closer to Ray. "He owned the building."

"He was just the managing agent."

"He was the only one we paid rent to."

"And before he took over?" asked Ray.

"He was here when we moved in. Nineteen forty nine. After my first child married."

"I'm sorry to have bothered you then," said Ray. "But they told me you were the oldest tenant in the building."

"I am," said Mrs. Rosenthal. "The older ones all died off years ago. I don't know how I got this far. They were all younger."

"You're doing okay. Thanks for the coffee."

"You don't have to go so soon."

"I'm busy and this has been a dead end. If anyone could have helped me it would have been you."

Mrs. Rosenthal rose and took Ray's hand. "Have you spoken to Mrs. Baron?"

"Who?"

"My neighbor," said Mrs. Rosenthal. "Across the hall. You should meet her anyway. You said you were single."

"I'm really not interested in meeting anyone at the moment."

"She can help you. She knows hundreds of stories about the building. She was here years before me."

"I thought you were the oldest tenant?" asked Ray.

"Oldest, yes, but she lived here the longest. Talk to her." Mrs. Rosenthal led Ray through the front door of her apartment and across the hall to the door of 11-A where she rang the bell. Ray smiled at Mrs. Rosenthal, heard footsteps, and then a muffled voice on the other side of the door asked, "Who is it?"

"Mrs. Rosenthal. I have a handsome young man here who I would like you to meet."

Ray had to smile again. The door of 11-A opened a crack and a dark haired, youngish woman, who Ray found to be attractive, looked out cautiously. She then opened the door wide, looked from Mrs. Rosenthal to Ray, and asked, "You're not a salesman?"

"He's interested in the building," said Mrs. Rosenthal.

"Oh," she replied. "Another writer. You think people will tire of the Crowell family after all these years."

"I am not a writer. My name is Ray Warren and I'm an attorney Mrs. ...."

"Baron," said the woman.

"I'm trying to track down a former tenant. An estate matter to his benefit." Ray handed Mrs. Baron one of his business cards. She glanced at it quickly and then said, "Why don't you both come in."

Mrs. Rosenthal hung back. "You talk to him alone. I'm waiting for a telephone call from my daughter-in-law. He's a nice young man. Divorced. Just right for you."

"You're embarrassing both of us," said Mrs. Baron.

"Why? He's a nice fellow. I'll ring your bell after I get the call."

"You do that," said Ray, "and I'll buy both you girls dinner for your help."

"I'll take you up on that," said Mrs. Rosenthal. Ray entered Mrs. Baron's apartment and waited for her to close the hall door before he said, "I won't take up too much of your time. Obviously your neighbor is mistaken, she's a nice old lady, but—"

"But what?"

"She said that you would know something about the building."

"I'm the tenant that lived here the longest."

"You're kidding!"

"If forty seven years long enough for you? Subtracting time out and a short marriage? I still keep my ex-husband's name but it's actually Cohen."

"Come on?" said Ray not taking her for a day over thirty five.

"I was brought here directly from the maternity hospital," she said, pouring out two drinks on her countertop without asking. "When my husband left me I moved back in with my mother. You can't beat rent control."

Ray could tell from the way she handled her scotch and water that she was an alcoholic. He felt sorry for her. She talked on and on about the building as if it were the only thing in the world that interested her. Ray finally had to cut in on her conversation and asked, "Back to the reason for my visit. I'm trying to track down a former tenant. The Ritter family," said Ray using the X-factor name again.

Mrs. Baron finished her drink in one swallow and then said slowly, "It wasn't their name."

"What was it then?"

Mrs. Baron's eyes seemed to mist over and she took even longer answering. "It was a Hungarian sounding name. Yes, Hungarian. My mother always referred to the wife as that Hungarian woman. The moved in just after the end of the war in Europe. The woman was very pretty. I remember her distinctly. I don't think I ever saw her husband." She said suddenly, "If it's an estate matter, how come you don't know their correct name? It wasn't Ritter!"

"Mr. Geisler had a number of distant relatives. That's what's making this case so difficult," replied Ray. With great caution he added, "I only assumed that it was Ritter."

"No, you didn't assume anything. You're playing a game with me! You know their name."

"I assure you I don't. And, I think you'd better go easy on that drink."

"Don't tell me what to do. This is my apartment."

"I'm only trying to help—"

"You're a liar!"

Ray got up from his chair with the intention of leaving, but Mrs. Baron said suddenly, "You were in the army during the war?"

"Yes, of course. Wasn't everybody?"

"An officer!"

"Yes."

"You had something to do with tanks!"

Ray settled back into his chair, picked up his drink, and said, "Go on!"

"You were in Germany," said Mrs. Baron.

"Right again!" said Ray. "What are you? A psychic?"

"I was beginning to think that I was a moment ago," said Mrs. Baron coldly. "You attracted me when I first saw you in the hall. I began to feel like a little girl again. Then I got this weird feeling of *deja vu* as we've been through it all before. We have, Mr. Warren."

"We have what?" asked Ray.

"Met before."

"No way," said Ray.

"We did! Right in this room. I opened the door for you as I did just before. You asked my mother the same questions you're asking today."

"Go on," said Ray.

"You came to the door asking if there were any new tenants in the building. Refugees. You didn't know their names back then either. You said it was an estate matter. My mother told you everything. My brother was very impressed with your campaign ribbons. He pestered you with questions. You told him that you commanded a tank company and that you were a lawyer. Right? Mr. Warren, don't look at me as if I'm crazy."

"Please, Mrs. Baron, I'm just a little stunned. You're not crazy. There was somebody here after the war, but it wasn't me.... Did he find the people he was looking for?"

"Of course he did, they lived right across the hall in the apartment Mrs. Rosenthal has now. You were in there."

"One more question, Mrs. Baron! Did the refugees move out right after the officer called on them?"

"If I recall correctly, yes!" said Mrs. Baron. "The next day."

"You don't know how helpful you've been, Mrs. Baron," said Ray excitedly. "And I haven't forgotten that dinner, but we'll have to put it off for another night."

## 33

Ray brought Morris to a safe house, a duplex apartment in a luxury brownstone on East 74th Street, to tell Braddock what he knew of the story.

The aging lawyer, taking the whole affair somewhat humorously, settled into a plush sofa and said, "I'll try to be helpful. I still haven't the slightest idea what you fellows can make out of it."

"That's our business, Captain," said Ray. "Tell my friend here the whole thing right from the beginning."

"The entire story? It's rather long."

"Please," said Braddock. "I haven't the slightest idea what you have for us. All I know is that Ray thought it was important enough to bring me up from Washington and he knows how much I hate New York."

Morris looked at Ray with a puzzled expression. "You didn't tell him anything?"

Ray said, "I wanted him to hear it straight from the horse's mouth."

"I'm rather embarrassed," said Morris managing a youthful blush.

"We're all friends here," said Braddock reaching into his jacket pocket for his pipe.

"It was just money. I was always interested in the quick buck," said Morris looking down at his drink with a great sadness. "No, I wouldn't say that. I wasn't always interested in money. I got the bug after I transferred over to the J. A. G. during the occupation. I saw a lot of fellows raking it in. The black-market, mostly penny-ante deals. Being a lawyer I figured that if I was going to stick my neck out, it would have to be for a bundle. I was concerned for a time with the repatriation of American assets frozen in Axis countries." Morris handed his drink to Ray for a refill. "I mainly dealt with matters pertaining to the entertainment industry; collection of royalties, frozen bank accounts, so on and so forth. The Hollywood companies sent people over to work with me and they were free with a dollar. I was on the payroll, under the table of course, of three studios while I was still in uniform. I wasn't hurting anyone and still doing my job."

Ray handed Morris a fresh drink. "It was a joy ride. The Germans did all of my work for me. They kept excellent records. None of my determinations were ever disputed. Then a strange case came across my desk. A small company, Uber Films. No one in the States seemed to have heard of it or claimed it, but it was seized by the Nazi government as U.S. property. It hasn't been active since Thirty Three and it didn't have any assets except a couple of terrible old Bavarian motion picture comedies. Terrible films, but innocuous enough for the censors back then. A German distributor wanted to release them. They had no film product at the time. I doubted that the company was American owned, probably Jewish I thought, but the distributor insisted that Crowell Collier was the owner. I informed the Collier Foundation. They chose to ignore the matter."

"Was Max Geisler in any of the films?" asked Ray.

"All of them." Taking another sip of his drink, Morris continued, "There were thirty prints of each feature sitting in a warehouse and a sharp Kraut ready to pay hard currency for them. To resolve the matter legally would have taken years. I didn't like the idea of a German sitting on a pile of Swiss Francs he was itching to part with, so I had the films released to him."

"Just like that?" asked Braddock.

"Well, he did have a letter signed by Crowell Collier selling Uber Films to him. I didn't dispute it. I wasn't a handwriting expert."

"Who signed it?"

"My sergeant. I always cut in all the boys in my office. After that I got even more ambitious. I recalled the story about Crowell stealing from his mother and I began to envision a hidden fortune in Europe, mine for the taking."

"Did you find it?" asked Braddock.

"The works!" said Morris.

"Beautiful," said Braddock. "How much did you end up with?"

"Nothing!" said Morris. "I discovered that Crowell had transferred or sold everything to one man. A Hungarian or Austrian named Kuris, a resident of Munich. All the documents were in order. I was ready to drop my quest for riches when I noticed that some of them were dated after Crowell's disappearance. Then I had an expert look at them. Kuris's and Crowell's signatures were identical. I assumed that Kuris had gotten the same idea I had years before and beaten me to the punch. I decided to track him down and threaten him with the powers of the J.A.G. if he didn't cut me in. I couldn't find him in Europe. Then the idea hit me, if he snatched all of Crowell's property he also had the building on West Eighty Third Street. So my visit to .... "

"The Cohens!" said Ray.

"The Cohens! Yes, they had some children."

"Did you find Kuris?" asked Braddock.

"In a way, yes. I used a ruse to get into the building. The Cohens were the only ones at home who could be of help. They directed me across the hall. The door was opened by a very beautiful, young woman. I asked to speak to the gentleman of the house. My uniform caused her to start. She refused to let me in."

"But you did get in?" asked Braddock.

"Forced my way in."

"Was the man Kuris?" asked Braddock.

"I didn't know what Kuris looked like. But this fellow had a beard and a hair piece. He was much older than his wife."

"Any conversation would have been moot at that point. I apologized and left. I had seen enough to know that my road to riches had hit a dead end. When I returned to my hotel I reviewed the material I had collected on Kuris. Almost the same date of birth, physical description, and handwriting as Crowell. Crowell's signature was authentic. It was he who forged Kuris's. Just to double check I went further into Kuris's background when I returned to Europe. He was killed early in World War One and stayed dead until Crowell resurrected him in Nineteen Eighteen."

Ray asked Morris, "Why didn't you tell this to Simon?"

"He would have laughed at me for wasting my time on another wild goose chase. Nothing I've ever done has turned out well."

## 34

When he and Ray got back to Washington, Braddock said, "What if your friend Morris is lying?"

"Morris, why?"

"If he was as money hungry as he said he could have capitalized on finding Crowell Collier."

"Ankhorn never capitalized on anything! He's a dreamer. He's the most unaccomplished person I ever met."

"Wine, women, and song!" said Braddock.

"And Simon Blake!"

"Simon Blake?" asked Braddock.

"Simon always came to the Captain's rescue," said Ray. "If the old man had to sink or swim a couple of times after the war he would have made something of himself."

Braddock took a puff on his pipe and then said, "What if Crowell Collier turns up in a nursing home?"

"He's not alive. I've read everything there is to read about him. He was a boozer and never did a lick of exercise. Unless, which is improbable, he took a complete turnaround after he lit out on Momma and became a health freak."

Braddock asked, "Children? If I knew I was a son of Crowell Collier, I'd—"

"Be at the foundation with a shopping bag as soon as you were old enough to walk. If there were any kids, they don't know who poppa really was. The way I read it, he hid out from Momma in Europe with some broad, got tired of her when she aged, got caught up in the war, and then pulled a few strings to get admitted back into the States as soon as the shooting stopped with a new *amorata*. He didn't start having kids at fifty nine."

"I'll buy that," said Braddock.

"We'll have to get that girl to revise the script. Crowell takes the name Kuris and then becomes a big man in the party."

"Kuris? I don't remember any Kuris. We can't rewrite every history book in the world."

"Okay!" said Ray. "Kuris was killed in the big war. Crowell picks up a couple of identities in addition to his. Give me a name, I'm not up on the whole Nazi party."

"Martin Borman!"

"That's a little too steep."

"If we're going to go down the tubes with this, we may as well go down with a splash. Scratch Borman and put in Rudolph Hess."

"He's still alive."

"That's where the poker face comes in," said Braddock. "Of course he'll deny it, but if our story was true, so would Crowell Collier."

## 35

Jane Scott stood in front of the full length, closet mirror knotting the shoulder throngs of her blouse. Simon couldn't keep his eyes off of her. She had yet to put on her skirt and was only clad in sheer panty hose below the waist. Simon put down his drink and said, "Come here!"

Jane, totally committed to the task of leveling her neckline, replied, "I'm getting dressed. We're going out to dinner aren't we?"

"Come here!"

"Don't tell me I'm turning you on?"

"What else?"

Jane stepped into a narrow, off white skirt and draped her blouse over it carefully. "I don't see what you see in me. I'm thirty. My tits aren't much."

"Come here," said Simon for the third time.

Jane sat at the opposite end of the room. She never seemed to cross her legs, yet always showed a lot of thigh. She told Simon, "Say something! Just don't stare at me."

"Okay!" said Simon beaming with enchantment. "How's the script coming?"

"The rewrite? It may make money. They brought in a guy from Hollywood to work with me. I have to admit he's a genius. I don't really think that I've been contributing much more than some research, but the money's worth it."

"I'd like to hear my son Sam say something like that. And I'm glad you haven't mentioned the word art once since I met you."

"It's not my bag. Neither is screen writing. I'm a biographer. I can't wait to wrap up the movie project. I have another book going."

"About what?" asked Simon.

"You," said Jane.

Simon laughed. "Of course," he said, "you're pulling my leg." With a yawn he added, "You know, some guy wanted to write a book about me once. He wanted twenty grand up front. What a jiggle."

"I've already talked to my publisher. You're best seller material."

Simon didn't answer. Jane finally said, "Well?"

Simon took a deep breath and then said, "I would like a book about my old tank outfit."

"World War Two doesn't sell anymore. They want a success book."

"I hit the beach with them at Normandy and went all the way to Munich. We saw a lot of combat."

"Wounded twice and awarded a Silver Star. The only thing anybody's interested in is how you made your money."

"Crap!" said Simon getting up from his seat. "Let's get something to eat."

"We'll give a chapter to the war—"

"A chapter? Do you know how many tanks I had shot out from under me?"

"Three," said Jane

"Let's go. I'm hungry. No one would be interested in a book about me."

"You're a billionaire."

"On paper, not cold cash."

"Readers don't know the difference."

"It would be boring, Jane. All I did was work my ass off. Do you know that I can frame a house, lay out plumbing, run BX cable? I did it all when I couldn't afford to hire anyone."

"You didn't do it for very long. You came out of the army in Forty five. Five years after the war, you're worth millions. A typical, American, success story! Not much different than Armanda Collier's."

"Hard work, kid!"

"I work very hard and there's isn't one chance in a hundred that'll I'll see a million dollars in my lifetime. Where did you get your start-up capital from? Not your family. Your father had a broken down luggage shop on Seventh Avenue. He never saw more than five thousand a year in his life."

"I pulled a couple of jiggles."

"That's what people want to read about."

"You have a better chance of finding Crowell Collier than unraveling any of my early deals."

## 36

The Judge opened the envelope on his desk and discovered that it contained a neatly folded page of newsprint in German. He unfolded it and laid it out flat on his desk. One of the advertisements Simon had placed was outlined in red and a large question mark was written next to it. The Judge's initial reaction was that Simon had sent the advertisement just to irk him, but a second look at the envelope told him otherwise. It bore a Munich postmark but lacked a return address.

Binney picked up his private telephone, referred to the number on the back of his watch with the aid of his magnifying glass, dialed Control, and asked quickly, "Would you know why I would receive correspondence from Germany regarding the Max Geislers?"

"I think we have a unit in Munich," replied Control.

"How can I contact them?" asked the Judge.

"I don't know, sir!" was the reply. "Did they give you a procedure book?"

"They're all dead!" shouted Binney. "I'm the only one left and they never gave me a damn thing." The Judge slammed down the telephone and shook his head. *God damn it, why is Blake causing all this trouble? Could it be possible that he was part of White Wash all along? No! Steinhoffen was an accident. It couldn't have been part of the operation. It would have been insane.*

## 37

Let's start at the very beginning, thought the Judge. April Twenty-fourth, Nineteen Forty Five. They didn't parachute me into Germany, I flew there in the belly of a modified Mosquito piloted by a serious young R.A.F. officer who had no idea why I was being delivered deep inside the enemy's homeland that late in the war. He was a good pilot, as good as they came. He landed in full dark on a highway thirty miles south of Munich.

The atmosphere of high adventure lasted less than fifty seconds after I tumbled out of the belly of the Mosquito clutching two suitcases, one containing the money I was to hand over to Lily. I had not gone more than a few feet when I heard the honk of a car horn and I was caught in the headlights of a large touring automobile which started with a lurch and lumbered out of a side road towards me. The car was a Duesenberg in immaculate condition.

I said, "*Gueten morgen*," as the Duesenberg pulled up alongside of me, casually tossed my luggage into the back seat, and got into the front. Lily was behind the wheel. I had expected her, but not that soon. She turned off the engine and said in English, "Long time, no see, Fossie."

"I'd like to kill you, but for the moment, let's get on with it," I replied. "And, for God's sake, speak German."

"Come on, Fossie, I haven't spoken English in years. It's okay, kiddo! The fix is in and no one is going to hear us way out here in the sticks." Lily gave me a playful punch on the shoulder, started up the car, and drove off in the direction of Munich. "This is better than the train, kiddo! They would have nabbed you in no time. Your German is for the birds."

I replied, "I still prefer that we spoke in that language. I need the opportunity to practice and you have a terrible Broadway accent which I find particularly grating. It's out of date, Lily! It went out of style with prohibition."

Lilly threw me a kiss, ignored my statement completely, and said, "Tell me what you think, Fossie? Still beautiful? Pretty good for an old woman?"

I had to admit that she was still gorgeous, extremely so. She had a new air about her, a grand air. It was only when she spoke English that the teenager in her came through. I said, "I'm getting out of this car if you don't speak German."

"Come on Fossie, stop playing war games. Jesus Christ, how I miss talking to another American."

"Lilly, you barely spent any time in the United States."

"I am an American citizen twice over, Fossie. And, you know how I miss New York. Forty second Street! The Broadway shows! Central Park!"

"Speak German!"

"Fossie, don't take me for a bean bag. Do you actually think I'm going to speak English if we're stopped? Please, Fossie, it's been so long. Please?" She suddenly changed the subject and asked, "The old lady kicked the bucket, didn't she?"

"The news isn't just getting to you, is it?"

"Of course not! You probably did well by her."

"No, Crowell got everything," I replied.

"Well, he is her son."

"Is?"

"Why are you asking that? Didn't you figure it all out already?"

"There wasn't much to figure."

She was silent for a long time and then she said, "In that case let's drop the subject. You have a job to do here and you may get the wrong ideas. Fossie, believe me, it was the old lady's fault."

"Bull!"

She said commandingly in German, "Did you bring the money?"

"Of course!"

"You understand that no matter what you think, you're the only man in the world I can trust."

"I understand."

"I'm doing this for money alone."

"A bargain is a bargain. I'll keep my end of the agreement."

"I want to get away from here clean. I don't trust your people all that much. If they get their hands on those fuel rods before I get paid and before I'm clear of Europe, I'm a dead woman."

"Just how high a ranking Nazi are you?"

Lily laughed and reverted to English. "Me? I'm not even a member of the party. I just made all the wrong friends over here, that's all."

"And now they're losing."

"Of course they're losing. They're a bunch of idiots. I could tell you things that you won't believe. The whole mob, Fossie! Goring, Hitler—"

"Hitler? How close are you to him?"

"Friends!"

"You mean you're sleeping with him."

"Me? I'm an old lady. He likes young girls."

"Then you found them for him."

"He doesn't need any help," laughed Lily. She patted me on the knee and said, "You'll keep your word, Fossie, I know. The deal goes through on the up and up—no funny business. I'm smarter than you are Fossie, remember that. That's why Crowell liked me. I was as sharp as his mother."

"Eviler, not smarter."

"Have you been looking after my investments in New York?"

"Investments?"

"The apartment building?"

"What apartment building?"

"West Eighty Third Street," she said with a glance out of the side of her eye.

"Oh, that building. I didn't know you owned that building."

"Half! You've been putting my share aside. Right?"

"I've been putting away a hundred percent of the income. I was given no instructions how to disburse it."

"I'm giving you instructions now."

"You can't. I have to hear from a majority of stockholders."

"You're the other stockholder now."

"I am not."

"Nobody knows for sure. You deserve to make a few bucks."

"I am not the other stockholder."

"Don't play games. Crowell was."

"If Crowell was the other stockholder, I will have to inform the Armanda Collier Foundation."

"It was that other person, what was the name, Kuris. Kuris, Crowell Collier, what does it matter. One and the same person."

"What happened to Crowell Collier?"

Lily slammed on the brakes and brought the car to an abrupt halt. "You know what happened to him!"

I said, "As far as I know, he married you and went to live in Germany."

"Okay, Fossie. We'll play it that way. Forget about the building! We're approaching a checkpoint. The fix is in, but we may run into some nut Nazi who wouldn't understand. If you have to speak German try to keep it down to *Ja* or *Nein*. Your papers will talk for you."

I said, "I hope the forgers back in the States knew what they were doing."

"Forgers?" laughed Lily as she started the car up again. "Your papers were issued in Berlin and signed by Himmler himself."

## 38

It was dawn as we entered Munich and drove along Prinzregenten towards the Iser. The city was one vast burned out ruin. "Did you thank Hitler for that?" I asked Lily.

"For what?" she replied.

"For destroying your home town?"

"The British and the Americans did that," she said without much concern.

"They didn't start the war."

"What can you do, Fossie?" she shrugged. "The Nazis have no class." Instead of continuing across the Isar, Lily turned left and drove along the river to an apartment building on a rise overlooking the Deutsches Museum. A stray bomb had destroyed a similar structure a little way down the street, but, otherwise, the neighborhood looked relatively intact. Lily pointed to the gutted ruin and said, "That's a mistake. They were told not to bomb near me."

She stopped the car around the corner from her building, got out, and removed a heavy padlock from a large wooden gate leading to a narrow mews at the building's rear. She then carefully backed the Duesenberg into the mews and relocked the gate. She whispered in English, "My getaway car." In German she said, "Germany used to be so nice and orderly. You can't trust anyone these days."

I followed her into the building by a rear door. As she turned on the hall light she said, "I'm in the back with a view of the river. Just like West Eighty Third Street."

As I followed her up the staircase she apologized for the lack of an elevator as if I were a weekend guest. Stopping in front of the door of her apartment she asked, "There's no funny business with the money? It's good stuff?"

"It's good stuff," I said mimicking her.

"Did you count it?"

"Of course I did. I had to sign for it."

"What's good enough for you is good enough for me. It's all I have in the world, Fossie. The rest is all toilet paper, German marks, and real estate with bomb holes in it. Lily unlocked the front door and held it open for me. "I'll show you the bedroom."

"Let's just conclude our business," I said as I followed her inside through a long, dark hallway. "I have precise instructions about a pension in Schwabbing."

Lily put a finger to her lips and motioned me into a rather sparsely furnished bedroom. She flicked on an overhead light and whispered, "I have another guest."

"I have precise instructions—"

"It was only if I didn't pick you up when I landed. It's a flea bag, really, Fossie, and you wouldn't have lasted twenty four hours with your German. Please! Wash up! I want you to meet someone."

As I shaved I came to the conclusion that her guest was the key man in operation White Wash. A high ranking Nazi or General Staff Officer who had started working with us as soon as he had seen the handwriting on the wall. Lily called to me from the door of the living room, "Fossie, he wants to talk to you now. He doesn't have much time."

"Let me put on my jacket and get rid of this." I held up the pouch containing my toilet articles.

"It's not that formal, come on!" Lily came down the long hall, took my arm, escorted me back to the living room and said in German, "Fossie, I'd like you to meet a friend of mine, Adolph Hitler."

## 39

I turned to Lily with a patronizing smile as if I was about to ask how she dare assume that I would be jolted by a remark like that. She read my thoughts and stepping forward towards a figure seated deep in blackout curtained room, "My Führer .... Herr Doctor-Colonel J. Foster Binney."

I hung in air, speechless, as the figure rose shakily from a chair in the darkened room, took a step forward, and said, "In this situation it's just Colonel Binney. Correct, yes?" He extended his hand as if he expected me to shake it. My mind went completely blank. I hadn't the slightest idea how to react. When I was able to organize a train of thought, I knew that orders or not, I would kill the bastard on the spot.

The Führer snapped, "Turn on the lights. I have to make sure."

"It's Herr Binney," replied Lily.

He said again, "I have to make sure."

"Please," said Lily, "believe me. It's Judge Binney."

"The lights!"

Lily turned on the lights. I couldn't believe my eyes. I was the same man I had seen in all the newsreels only this time much less arrogant. He came forward and studied my face. "Yes! Colonel Binney!"

When I got my voice back up again I said, "How the hell would you know? You've never seen me before."

"Photographs! I picked you personally from the American Forces. A man of honor. If I only had more men like you around me we wouldn't have to go through this." He turned his back on me, returned to his seat, and said, "Turn off the light!"

"You bastard," I shouted at him. "You've ruined this country, caused the death of millions, and, now you're trying to make a deal to save your own skin!" I was about to leap across the room and strangle him when I heard laughter behind me. I jerked my head around to discover Lily clutching her stomach in hysterics. She said between gasps of laughter, "Relax Fossie, it's only Max."

"Max?" I screamed.

Lily forced herself to stop laughing and put a warning finger to her lips. "Max Geisler the comedian. Look!" She went to the window, drew the blackout curtains, and let the full morning sun into the room. "Max Geisler the comedian. He does a very good impression, yes?"

The man in the chair was just as shaken as I was. He tried to smile. He said, "I had to look at your face. I thought Lily was playing a joke on me, not you. I'm sorry! It wasn't very funny." He got to his feet slowly. "It's been very bad for Jews here. Lily has been looking out for me. Now, I must go to bed. I didn't sleep last night." He turned and went off into the hall.

I counted to ten before slapping Lily. "Don't you know this is not a game?"

She gasped, "I'm sorry!"

"Let's just get it over with, okay?"

"You'll see the stuff this afternoon. At the University. Then let's get rid of each other."

"Fine! Can we trust Max?"

"Max? Don't worry about Maxi. He'll keep his mouth shut. They'd kill him sooner than they would you."

"How come you're taking the risk of hiding him?"

"He was my first boyfriend. Before Crowell."

"Why didn't you just get him out of the country? You have the contacts."

"He didn't want to go until it was too late. This is all he knows. He has trouble with English."

As I started out of the room she said, "One more thing, Fossie. Please? You're not going to try to kill me?"

"Not until it's all over."

"Good! You'll never find me after this is all over."

"I'm sure Donavan made arrangements to see to that. I only hope they did as much to protect me. There's no reason to keep me alive after the signals are off."

"President Roosevelt made the arrangement just before he died. He said that you were a personal friend of his and as far as he was concerned, he would blow Germany off the face of the earth if one hair of your head was touched. You know, not one bomb will fall on Munich or any German city that you are in. You're the key man in Wish Wash."

"It's White Wash and you'd better remember that when you drive through our lines in that fancy car of yours. Our boys do something I highly approve of—they shoot people for bad English."

## 40

When I awoke, Lily was dressed and waiting for me. I insisted, "Can we resolve your part of the business immediately?"

"Of course, Fossie. I'm behind schedule. We have an appointment at the University this afternoon. You'll see what you have to see. Being the money with you and your luggage. You won't be coming back here."

On the street she turned away from the mews where she had parked the Duesenberg explaining, "I'm saving my beauty. It will be too conspicuous during the day. Somebody may try to requisition it by force. We'll take the tram."

There was one thing I had to admire about the Germans. Munich was almost totally obliterated, yet the city seemed to function normally if not with great bustle. We rode the tram across the river and then walked through the rubble toward the University. Lily turned off onto Teresein Street and asked, "A little lunch, Fossie? You must be starved."

"I'd rather get on with our business."

"You didn't have any breakfast. Come on, Fossie, lunch on me. Our appointment isn't until three o'clock. Venison? Good coffee? The owner has good connections."

I wasn't exactly on a tour, but lunch seemed reasonable. I adored venison and couldn't go long without coffee. Lily led me past a row of heavily damaged buildings into a basement cafe packed with affluent businessmen, Wehrmacht, SS, and Luftwaffe officers. Her choice of an eating spot didn't rattle me. It was the last place anyone would look for a spy in Munich.

A portly waitress in a black skirt and peasant blouse greeted Lily gruffly and escorted us to a table. A Luftwaffe Captain with only one leg was making a pitiful mess of Strauss at the keys of an upright piano against one wall. With a smug look I ordered two coffees in acceptable German. Lily said, "You're German isn't that bad at all."

When the coffee came, I remarked, "Pretty good."

Lily replied, "I told you so," in English.

I almost jumped out of my chair. The nearest German officer was close enough to rub against my shoulder. Lily covered her mouth and giggled. To remain on the safe side, I decided to remain mute for the rest of the meal when a singularly handsome blonde young man in an SS uniform entered the cafe, greeted a number of his friends, and after spotting Lily, hurried to our table and said loudly, "Lily, darling."

She rose and embraced him. "Rolph, please join us for lunch." He removed the fourth chair at our table and placed it by the piano. He said, "I don't want any stranger sitting with us, yes?" He clicked his heels, bowed to me, and said, "First Lieutenant Rolph Liebhomm."

I rose to introduce myself under my cover name not knowing if the newcomer was part of White Wash or if Lily was playing another practical joke. She said, "My dear old friend Rolph, I would like you to meet an older and dearer friend of mine. Colonel Foster Binney of the American paratroopers."

The SS officer was more shocked by her words than I was. He actually gulped. He then reached over and shook my hand, patted Lily on the head, and said, "Please, darling not in here. There are people in this place without a sense of humor."

I said in German, "Lily, he's right. Every one's on edge with the war going so badly."

Rolph took a seat and banged on the table for service. Lily said to me, "You don't have to worry. Rolph wouldn't hurt a fly." She pulled up his arm so I could see the insignia on his sleeve. "Just honorary SS All they do is entertain the troops."

"Not only! We've been activated for combat," said Rolph.

"General Eisenhower won't lose any sleep over it if you want the truth," said Lily.

Rolph asked me, "What was your name again? I didn't quite get it."

"Colonel Binney," said Lily, "of the American army."

"I'm sorry I asked," replied Rolph, slapping a hand to his forehead. "Please, let's eat."

Handing me the menu, Lily said, "Why don't you order for us?"

After I did so, Lily asked Rolph, "What do you think of my friend's German?"

"He has an accent," said Rolph.

"What kind of accent?"

"Who knows? Prussian. In Berlin they say I have an accent." Turning to me he asked, "Where are you from?"

Lily said quickly, "Abrusehoffen on the North Sea."

"Ah, a small town," said Rolph. "I'm from right here in Munich. A one hundred percent Bavarian and a Catholic. Abrusehoffen? My films must play there."

"I loved all of them," I said, not quite sure that the handsome young man could be that dense.

"Especially the ones with Max Geisler," said Lily.

Rolph whispered, "Lily, I wish you wouldn't mention that name in here." He looked around the room and then whispered, "When the Americans are really here they'll all love him again."

Lily said, "I introduced the Colonel to Max."

"Max, who?" Rolph had turned his attention to flirting with two office girls who had just entered.

"Max Geisler!"

"Come on, please. Old Max got out a long time ago. Unless you tell me he arrived from America today with your friend here."

"No, he's hiding in the city."

"Maxi? You're kidding me. All these years? I thought he was in Hollywood with the other Jews."

"This is true, I tell you."

Rolph smiled, going along with it. "Of course. Max knew he wouldn't have done well over there. He was too regional for the Americans. He never even did business in Berlin. If the Gestapo doesn't get their hands on him before the Americans arrive, I'll have to talk to him. We'll have to organize a cabaret."

Lily said, "Maxi won't be available. The Colonel here is from Hollywood on a very delicate matter concerning the movies."

"Hollywood?"

"He parachuted in to make sure the Americans got all our good talent before the Russians."

Rolph turned to me and studied my face. "You know, you do have an English accent."

"What have I been telling you all along," said Lily. "But there's no hope for you, so don't pester him."

"No hope? Me? I was offered Hollywood employment once. A personal representative of Louis B. Meyer. Of course I turned him down. I was doing too well and worried about my English. I don't have any."

"You're a party member and an SS man. You'll be hanged at soon as they come."

"As an actor I was forced to join the party. And the SS everybody joined. All we do now is guard public buildings."

"No hope," said Lily. "You're marked for death."

"Your friend hasn't heard me sing yet," said Rolph. "All is forgiven when Liebhomm sings." He got up and went to the piano.

I told Lily, "You're out of your mind."

"Rolph's harmless. I've been pulling his leg so long he doesn't know what to think and he's panicked about the war. He does have a beautiful voice. Listen!"

Rolph played an arpeggio and, in a full operatic tenor, started singing, "Home on the Range" in German.

I said to Lily, "He forgot to dedicate it to our late President and myself."

"Take it easy," said Lily. "It's for the crowd. They love cowboy songs in Munich."

# 41

The portion of my mission that involved a visit to the University seemed rational enough. Lily introduced me to the physicist who explained his motivations for turning the Magnetic Fuel Rods over to the United States. He was violently anti-Communist and wanted to see the material kept out of the Russian's hands. He said, "The rods have unlimited potential! They could have won the war for us, but Hitler doesn't believe in Atomic energy. And, without him, there's no co-operation from industry, no funds, nothing!"

Later, five keg-like containers were removed from a safe and the rods were shown to me. Lily asked, "Are you satisfied?"

I pushed the suitcase containing the money towards her. "I don't know what goes from here on in. I suspect arrangements have been made to transfer the material to my people?"

"Yes! All you have to do is signal them you're satisfied."

"I'll do that immediately."

"Then it's goodbye forever, Fossie. I'm sorry it has to be this way with a misunderstanding between us. Don't go back to my apartment. The pension is safe. I just didn't want you out of sight until I had my hands on the money. Give me an hour before you leave here." She threw me a kiss and hurried out the door with the suitcase.

A half hour later I walked along Leopold Street towards the Marienplatz until I came across a telephone kiosk. I dialed the radio operator's number and said some something like, "Is Carl there, this is his cousin just back from the front."

"Carl's dead, who are you?" asked the voice on the other end of the line. I gave him my approximate location. He then said, "I'm out in Kleinharden on Waldwisen Street. Can you manage?"

The radioman whose true name I've never learned was waiting for me at the tram terminal on Wurmtel Street. A short, nervous Bavarian with a shock of wild hair, he came up to me as I stepped off the tram and extended a hand to take my remaining suitcase. He said, "I'm Carl's brother," the pre-arranged identification code.

I replied, "Carl's dead."

He nodded and as we walked off in the direction of his house he said, "I sent the family off to relatives in the country."

I had first figured him for a Communist, but when we reached his little house on Wurmtel Street and secluded ourselves in an upstairs bedroom, he explained that he was newly recruited by the OSS out of a prisoner of war cage and only recently had become a dedicated anti-Nazi. He broke out a carton of Chesterfields and offered me a pack. "They came with the last air drop."

"Wouldn't it be dangerous to be caught with them?"

"Not any more than the radio. Besides, I don't think the Gestapo is concerned with us. They know it's all over for them."

"Where do you transmit from?"

"Here."

"All the time?"

"All the time!"

"What about triangulation?"

"My set's highly directional. Straight up to a plane almost every night. They would have to be as close to me as you are to intercept the signal or between the radio and the plane. I'm not worried. I think your transmission is the last."

"No! There are a few more pieces of information I have to secure."

"Such as?" he asked. "Maybe I can help you. There's no sense in duplicating efforts. You're not the only one I'm transmitting for."

I said, "The Alpine Redoubt and the Bavarian Action group."

"The redoubt is total fiction and the Bavarian Action group is in direct contact with General Patch. If I were you,

I'd just lay low. I wouldn't even try to make it back to the American lines. Please! There's only one thing I want from you. Call me every morning at eleven like clockwork until the Americans arrive. If I don't hear from you, I'll relocate. If you are caught I don't expect you to be a hero. Just hold out until five minutes after eleven. Please?"

My next stop was a small pension on Kaiser Place. I entered casually, inquired about a room, was given a key, and then trudged upstairs carrying my remaining suitcase. As soon as I opened the door of my room, two burley men in leather coats rose from the bed where they had been sitting. The older one said, "Gestapo! May we see your papers, please?"

Thinking I could bluff my way through, I handed him the papers I carried with a smile. The other man asked, "What's your name?"

I replied in German, and under the stress of the moment, I could have sworn I used an absolutely flawless German accent, "Christian Schnitzer."

They weren't impressed. I found myself facing two drawn pistols. The older man said, "Please, I think you'd better put your hands up."

"What's wrong with my papers?" I asked, raising my hands.

"They're bad forgeries. In any case, would you try again and tell us who you are? A name different from the one on your papers would be appreciated.

Lily had switched my identification while I had slept and then called the Gestapo and told them where I could be found. I should have expected as much, but I was stupid enough to once again trust her. I would have turned her in at that moment, but it would mean putting "White Wash" in jeopardy and lead to poor, old Max Geisler's arrest.

I was swung around, thrust against the wall, searched thoroughly and handcuffed. I didn't believe that I could hold up under torture or a truth serum and decided to use the "L" pill that had been secreted in a hollow tooth in my bridge at the first opportunity.

After searching my suitcase, they shoved me ahead of them down the stairs. Attempting to grab the proverbial last straw, I hastily concocted a story about being an escaped prisoner of war, but they weren't interested in listening to it. One of them said, "Of course you're a soldier. A deserter."

It wasn't until I was in their car that I gleaned from bits of their conversation that I had been exposed by a telephone call to their office and identified as an American spy. They thought the call was exaggerated. That I was a deserter from the German army. "And, obviously a senior officer, too," said the driver of the car, looking back at me.

They took me to a civilian police office and booked me as a vagrant found without proper papers and a suspected deserter. I was then forgotten for a moment in a communal cell containing about fifteen other prisoners. One nodded as I entered and then whispered to me, "They hung five of us yesterday. I wish the Americans would hurry up."

I cursed in German and found myself a seat on a bench in a corner. Pretending to be at odds with the world, I huddled over and pried the hollow tooth loose almost swallowing the "L" pill before I managed to bite down on it. I had a vision of my sons greeting me in another world even though I never believed that such a place existed. The cyanide tasted sour, but not as bad as I thought it would.

# 42

I rose less than an hour later covered with my own vomit in what I took to be a first aid room. My eyes focused on a man whom I assumed to be a doctor sniffing a portion of the rubber capsule I had bitten and shaking his head. With a shrug he said, "Whatever it is, it's not cyanide. They must be experimenting. He'll be all right. British?"

One of the beefy fellows that had arrested me answered, "I thought he was just another deserter .... but he did speak kind of funny. Like he was from the Rhineland."

"I think you have a British agent on your hands."

Another voice in the room said, "Didn't we get an alert to lookout for an American parachutist? A Colonel? It's been sitting on the desk for a week now. You boys may have hit it lucky."

"A week now?" It all, suddenly, came to me, the real purpose of my mission. They needed a superlative "Red Herring" and chose the internationally known Jurist, Foster Binney. It was ordained that I was to be apprehended by the Gestapo. For that reason, the "L" pill contained a relatively harmless substance. I was expected to break under torture and reveal the primary reason for my mission to Germany, the Magnetic Fuel Rods, which were totally worthless.

*Why?* I asked myself. The only answer that I could come up with at the moment was that the Japanese or the Russians were wasting their time with an atomic fuel project and Washington wanted to keep them doing so. I knew what was expected of me. To put up a show, take a severe beating, and then give them all the information they asked for.

The doctor, rather politely, suggested that I clean myself up. I did exactly that before being confined to a private cell after being relieved of my tie, belt, and shoelaces. It wasn't until the following morning that I found myself seated opposite an Inspector Strugg who rehashed the details of my arrest and then asked, "So, you are not Christian Schnitzer?"

"No." I gave him a story about being captured and then escaping and reminded him under that circumstance that I was within my rights to wear civilian clothes. I expected him to get down to the nitty gritty of asking the reason for my presence in Munich, but he never approached that subject. He shuffled papers like an assistant vice-president at a New England bank with very little authority. "From what I see here, your name is Binney and you are a Colonel in the U.S. Army. You wouldn't mind confirming that much would you?"

I nodded. He continued, "You parachuted into Germany within the last Forty Eight hours."

"No, I'm an escaped prisoner of war." I then assumed that he was going to get to the Magnetic Fuel Rods obliquely and make a better show of it than I would withholding the information until the limit of my physical endurance or my boredom threshold were reached.

"We have very good information that you're with the Office of Strategic Services on a highly classified mission. I would like to know your contacts here in Munich. You obviously have a radio operator, some means of contacting your forces?"

I didn't answer. Strugg said, "I understand your position. You are what we call a hero. A patriot! I'm concerned with our own people. The traitors. The woman who called us and turned you in? One of your people? They always are. Now, I can't see any reason you would mind giving up her name. I think you would be delighted."

I would have been more than delighted, but I answered, "I think you're wasting your time, Herr Inspector. You don't have to go all through that just to hang me." I added with a smile, "And I think you'd better make quick work of it before the American Army arrives."

"Possibly," said Strugg. "Then again you may be in the market for experienced police officers. My record is excellent. I started with the Bavarian State Police before they were nationalized."

*Jesus Christ*, I thought. *Here am I on the verge of being executed and this bastard is applying for a job.* To speed things up I said, pointedly, "Aren't you interested in my reason for being in Munich?"

Strugg replied, "No, I wouldn't expect you to condemn yourself. The fact that you are an espionage agent is clear. I'm more interested in uncovering the others in your ring. Your mission is best left to those who interpret such things. I'm just a simple cop."

"I think they have the wrong man for the job."

"You're very perceptive. I'm a criminal man, not a counter intelligence man."

"Then how did you get stuck with me?"

"Everyone else in this headquarters has found an excuse not to interrogate you. They don't know what the Allies would make out of it. Especially if you are hung immediately. I don't shirk responsibility."

I began to doubt my theory about operation "White Wash." Strugg wasn't the least bit concerned with the subject of my mission. He went strictly by the book and his only interest was tracking down a nest of spies. He was quite good at what he did for a living. When direct questioning led no place, he switched to conversational patter designed to trick bits of information out of me. He was also sure that the stenographer in the room got everything down precisely so that there was a record of him doing his job correctly for both his superiors and the conquerors.

"The woman, she was your contact here in Munich? There was obviously bad blood between you two. Why did she inform on you? Were you lovers?"

Before that subject was explored any further, an orderly handed Strugg a cable. He read it carefully, smiled, and then with a bit of embarrassment said, "Ah, hah! So you're Herr Doctor-Colonel Judge Foster Binney. You're very prominent in America. A friend of your late President. You were flown into Bavaria on an extremely confidential scientific mission."

When I heard scientific mission, my confidence in my reasoning abilities returned. I thought he was finally getting to the point, but he just put the cable aside and asked again, "The woman who called, who was she?"

When I still didn't answer, he rose and said, "We'll have to continue this tomorrow. My wife doesn't like me to be late for dinner .... Please sign this."

Strugg handed me a statement stating that I wasn't mistreated by the Gestapo. I signed and dated it. It was a fact up to that point. I returned to my cell aware that Strugg wasn't involved in "White Wash." He was just a cop, protecting his behind, fully aware of the consequences if I were rushed to the scaffold in the closing days of the war.

I was awoken at four o'clock in the morning and taken to Strugg's office to face a Lieutenant General in SS uniform. He shouted at me, "I'm Heinrich Müller, the commanding officer of the Gestapo! I've just read Inspector Strugg's transcript. Don't you understand? You're in a very perilous position. There is nothing left for you to do, but co-operate!"

"I don't know any woman,"

"What woman?" shouted Müller. "We must know the reason for you presence here in Munich. You're not a run of the mill espionage agent. You're a man of some prominence. What? What scientific matter brought you to Germany?"

Ah, hah! I thought. They're finally following the script. I replied, "I don't have the slightest idea what you're talking about."

Müller sputtered, "But?" just as Strugg came crashing into the room demanding to know what the hell was going on.

"This!" answered Müller, holding up the transcript. "The man is here on an important scientific mission. We are at our blackest hour. And, you're only concerned with his so called associates?"

"I'm a police officer. The question is, is he a spy or isn't he? Are there any other culprits? Who are these culprits? The rest is for military intelligence."

"And when did you expect to turn him over to military intelligence?"

"When I was finished with my part of the investigation!" Strugg shouted just as loud as Müller.

"You mean when the Americans are occupying this building. You're a defeatist, Strugg. You always left the dirty work to others. I don't know why Heydrich kept you on."

"Because I'm a professional police officer."

"Get out of here Strugg! I intend to question this prisoner myself, and, may I add, correctly!"

Strugg went to a typewriter, slipped a piece of paper in, and started banging away at the keys.

Müller's mouth dropped. He screamed, "What the hell do you think you're doing?"

"This man is my responsibility. I want written orders before I turn him over to you."

"Two copies!" shouted Müller. "One for the files and one for General Eisenhower?"

"I always make two copies," said Strugg seriously.

After Strugg had been given a receipt for me, Müller said, "Now that that petty civil servant is gone, let's not waste time. I must have the details of your scientific mission."

I wondered why the boys in Washington left this part of "White Wash" for me to figure out myself and hoped they hadn't selected me as the most important person they could afford to expend on the mission who's guaranteed to crack under torture. I decided to make a show of it and not reveal anything until I was actually close to breaking.

Müller started slapping me around rather halfheartedly. I rattled him by my indifference. He then called in two goons who were obviously old hands at abusing prisoners. They pulled me out of the chair I was sitting in and belted me a couple of times. When they had done over a thousand dollars' worth of damage to my teeth, Müller shouted, "Enough! Get out of here!"

Müller pulled up a chair next to me, offered me a cigarette, and whispered, "The war is over. Why must we go through all of this?"

I spit out a mouthful of blood and took on the countenance of a martyr.

"Please," said Müller, "you must have orders, special orders?"

I said, "I have no knowledge of a scientific mission."

Müller called his boys back in again. They threw me across the desk and started working me over with truncheons. I felt one of my ribs crack. Finally, Strugg stormed into the room and shouted at Müller, "You're going to kill him. "

Müller sputtered, "If I have to, I will."

"Allow me," said Strugg. "We have a special room for this." He called in two of the local cops and they dragged me down to the cellar, handcuffed my hands behind me, and gave me a good shot in the testicles. Strugg, close by at my side, said quietly, "Please, excuse me, but there is a science to it."

One of the bully boys said, "This is nothing special, Herr Colonel. Regular Municipal Police treatment, but not usually for gentlemen like yourself." He then gave me a shot in the kidney. The new team knew exactly what they were doing. When it got around to where they were holding my head under water and I was fighting their attempt to drown me, I decided that I had put up enough of a front, "Yes," I screamed. "I'm on a scientific mission."

"Will you make a statement now?" asked Strugg.

I nodded. He said, "Good, you're a strong, brave man. I hope you feel that you've retained your honor. I hope you live to return to your comrades and tell them that you were tortured by the Gestapo."

Back upstairs, Strugg told Müller, "He's ready to make a statement."

I wasn't in condition to repeat my name correctly, but Müller recalled most of the facts of my "confession" for me. He was most obviously part and parcel of "White Wash." I tried to implicate Lily and the physicist, but he muttered something about them being watched and insisted that we get down to the work being done on "Atomic engines." I skimmed over the subject, but the little I offered was enough to satisfy him. He said, "You put on a good show. Sign this!"

His aide took a prepared statement from a briefcase and handed it to me. It was my "confession," a twenty page transcript of technical information about atomic propulsion. I had read it before, in the States, when I was given the material as a study guide.

I was re-handcuffed and escorted out of the office. When we reached the lobby of the building, Strugg was waiting with his two underlings, a couple of Municipal Police in uniform, and a Catholic priest. The Priest shook me up. I thought they were going to go all the way with the drama and execute me just to make it look good. I was about to ask for a Protestant minister when Müller gave Strugg a dirty look and demanded, "What's all this?"

"Witnesses to the fact that the prisoner is leaving here alive."

"Good! Excellent!" said Müller. "The State Police will be reconstituted as it was before Heydrich in a few days and you'll be happy. You can even arrest me, if you can ever find me." He brushed Strugg aside and led us into the courtyard where he entered a waiting sedan. Two SS men in combat gear helped me into the back of an ambulance. We were on the road less than five minutes when it stopped, and a civilian got in. He took of my handcuffs and handed me the suitcase he was carrying. It contained two of the tailored battle uniforms I had left in Washington, a couple of extra shirts, socks, underwear, shaving things, and a box of my favorite Cuban cigars.

## 43

I lit one of the cigars and tried to sack out on a stretcher. Except for a puffy face, split lip, and sharp pain in my chest whenever I moved, I felt in great shape. My bridge hung awkwardly in my mouth, but I managed to bend it back into place. I didn't dare ask the SS up front where we were going, but by the direction of the rising sun I assumed Switzerland or Austria.

Some three hours later we turned onto a side road, went on for a bit, and then stopped. One of the SS boys opened the back door and helped me into an open area that looked like an outdoor cafe. I glanced up to see a faded sign that read, "Guest House Bloenberg."

I took a whiff of fresh, Alpine air and followed my guards inside the little hotel. The place gave me the impression of a rest camp rather than a military prison. There were a half a dozen SS in various states of undress lounging about the lobby. The scene was far from military. I wouldn't have allowed it in my own battalion. Not with prisoners around, anyway. One of my escorts asked an officer by the fireplace, "Are you the commander?"

The seated German, who had at least five years and fifty pounds on me, pointed to a door through which, as we drew closer, I could heard a lusty tenor vocalizing. The situation was so ludicrous and I laughed so hard that my cracked rib felt as if it had pierced my chest wall. The impromptu concert even got a smile out of the two Waffen SS guarding me. One of them knocked on the door and said, sarcastically, "Herr Commander. We have a prisoner for you."

Rolph Liebhomm came to the door in shirt sleeves and said, "What was that again?" before taking one look at me and almost urinating in his pants. One of my guards whipped out a piece of paper, explained that I was an important American espionage agent, and demanded a receipt. Rolph looked beyond the Waffen SS men to see if Lily was in sight as he thought he was being subjected to another practical joke. He then scribbled his name on the document and pulled a copy for himself.

The Waffen SS threw him a "*Heil* Hitler," turned on their heels and marched out of the guest house. It took Rolph a full five minutes to regain his composure and ask, "Would you like to come into my office?"

After closing the door, he pointed to a seat, and then said, cautiously, "She wasn't kidding, was she?"

I still had my cigar so I blew a puff of smoke in his face and then offered him one of my Upman's which he lit nervously. He said, "You didn't answer my question."

"Lily doesn't have a sense of humor that extends this far. Has Berlin fallen yet?"

"No yet .... Herr Colonel, you must understand that I'm a member of the Allgemeine SS, an honorary organization. We were just given this prison assignment yesterday."

"You're lucky that they didn't send you to the front. Where are we anyway?"

"I can't disclose that. Close to Austria. Quite nice isn't it? Mostly families came out this way before the war. Too quiet for me then. Now it's a camp for important prisoners. You, too, are lucky. We've been ordered to give exceptional care to our charges. We have an excellent cook."

"How about a little trout fishing?" I asked just to addle him a bit more.

"Trout fishing?" I had stopped him cold. "I'll have to ask about that. You can walk about the grounds with an escort. That is permitted."

"Good!" I replied. "Any other regulations I should know about?"

"We're working on them now!" Rolph rose, went to the door, and called off, "Erstein, come in here for a moment please."

A tall, balding fellow in his late thirties stuck his head in and said, "Yes, sir?"

"Are you working on the regulations?"

"Most certainly. It will take some time."

"Hurry!" said Rolph. Erstein clicked his heels and disappeared from view. Rolph said to me, "Erstein Is very careful about those things. He's a lawyer."

"It figures."

"The only thing for now, is that you're restricted to your room between ten at night and eight in the morning."

"Suits me fine. Is there a doctor and dentist available?"

"A doctor! I'll have to see about a dentist."

An orderly appeared to carry my suitcase and escort me upstairs to my room which was Number Two. The room adjoining it, number One, was occupied by an SS man who saluted as I came up the stairs. He said, "I'm the floor guard. THE Richard Heller. Playwright!" He then buried his nose in the book he had been reading.

Room Two had a large, double bed, a thick, down comforter, a fireplace, desk, and a postcard view of the Alps. It even had a private bath with hot water. I soaked for an hour, made myself presentable, and then went out to say hello to my fellow prisoners. Room Three was an actual cell that looked, by its size, as if it had been converted from a large linen closet. It had bare stone walls, no window at all, and a heavy steel door with a minuscule peephole. I assumed that it was for escape prone prisoners with less impressive credentials than myself. Room Four was much larger than the rest and had a modern bath. The rooms on the opposite side of the corridor, Five, Six, Seven, and Eight were identical to mine.

I went downstairs, knocked on Rolph's door, and asked him, "Can I meet the other prisoners?"

"You're the only one. We've been told to expect others shortly. I hope you're not bored. I am. We'll get up a little entertainment after dinner, Herr Judge."

"Herr Colonel," I reminded him.

He smiled and then motioning me forward whispered, "If what Lily said was true—that you're actually from Hollywood—then I would like you to look at my scrapbook."

"After the trout fishing!"

"Ah, the trout fishing. I checked with the Waffen SS Commander and he's making inquiries. The doctor is on his way."

"Who do I see about a cup of coffee?"

"You missed breakfast, but we can scrape something up. Let me introduce you to the boys."

Rolph's small outfit was made up of accountants, lawyers, writers, newspaper, and other non-military types dragged away from their desks in Munich. Rolph was worse than no commander at all and I dreaded the idea of the mismatched group of party members making an effort to defend the guest house or even trying to surrender it properly. A G.I. unit spotter seeing so many black uniforms in one place would blast the hell out of the area without bothering to ask questions. There wasn't one "Prisoner of War" sign in sight.

After the Doctor strapped me up and clipped the dangling bridge free from my mouth, I asked Rolph to take a walk around the grounds with me hoping to set him straight. The boys from the Waffen SS were still there, lounging by their ambulance with shit eating grins on their faces. They were probably the only effective guards in the place and they knew it. They followed us at a discrete distance to a ridge overlooking the guest house, Rolph said, "You get quite a nice view from up here."

I replied, "Correct! Don't you think you should have an emplacement up here rather than crowded around the buildings down there?"

"Why?" asked Rolph.

"Well, I would call it a military crest. It commands the whole area. If I were to defend this place, I certainly wouldn't want the enemy to get up here and fire down on me.

"It's not going to come to that, truly?"

"I hope not. There's no sense in all of us getting killed. I don't expect you to fire on the Americans, but it would be nice if you had a couple of men up here equipped with a big, white flag. It would be also nice if you saw that there were some P.W.s painted on the buildings immediately."

"To show there are prisoners of war here? I'll ask them if we can do that."

"And the emplacements down by the guest house are useless."

"Really?"

"They face a curve and they're on low ground. Move them to the highway."

"There's a Waffen SS unit near the highway." He lapsed into thought and then asked, "Do the Americans attack at night?"

"Not often, but you never know."

"Good!"

"Why, good?" I asked.

"The Waffen SS go off duty at night. That's why I have to lock you in. We don't have enough men."

"Get organized Rolph. You need some people behind the guest house and what about that other building?"

"That's our barrack. An annex. This place was expanding until the Nazis took over. I think the owner was Jewish."

"Get to it, Rolph! Big letters! P.W.! And lots of white flags in readiness."

"The Waffen SS set this camp up. I have no reason to doubt their planning."

"They're not winning the war. That's reason enough."

The odd collection of honorary SS men at the camp knew they were defeated yet something drove them on to continue playing soldier, a role they were relishing. At ten, after a fine dinner, when it appeared that Rolph was going to sing, I insisted on them following regulations and locking me in my room.

They couldn't. The floor guard explained, "We don't have a key to the lock on your door. We've been looking for it all afternoon. You'll give me your word?"

"Of course," I replied. "At my age you won't find me trudging through the foothills of the Alps on the run when I have a hot bath and a goose-down comforter." I borrowed a newspaper from him, returned to my room, built a fire, and read for a while. I then paced the corridor looking into the empty rooms as if that would fill them. It was then that I discovered that rooms were numbered out of order and that Room Two had recently been Room Three.

I paced off the length of the corridor carefully and found that all eight rooms were evenly spaced. Three hadn't been a utility closet at all. Its walls had been reinforced with at least three feet of additional masonry. As I examined it carefully, I heard a polite cough and turned to find the floor guard standing in the door behind me. He said, "What do you make out of it? We've been trying to figure it out ourselves."

I said, "I don't know, but it's obviously for a very special prisoner."

"Who?"

"I don't know, but I'd like to meet him. He must be extremely dangerous as far as you guys are concerned."

As I fell asleep I concluded Room Three was for some fanatical British Commando type officer. The sound of a plane landing in the vicinity woke me hours later. I heard footsteps in the hall. They stopped at my door. As I sat up in bed, I heard the sound of a key being placed in the lock and turned. After I heard the footsteps go off and down the stairs, I got up and tried the door. I couldn't budge it.

Then there was some muttered conversation in German, the tread of boots on the stairs, the sound of Room Three's door being swung open, and the sound of it being slammed shut again. A single set of footsteps went back down the stairs and I heard a motor vehicle starting up and driving away.

Driven by intense curiosity about the new arrival, I dressed hurriedly in the morning and rushed into the hall to discover Room Number Three guarded by two Waffen SS in combat uniforms and machine pistols. They clicked their heels and saluted, but when I approached the cell they said, "It is forbidden." I left well enough alone and went downstairs to find Rolph at breakfast with some of his men. I took a table by myself and motioned him over. He said, "Good morning, Herr Colonel. How's your rib?"

"Fine," I said.

"It's impossible!"

"What's impossible?"

"The re-deployment of forces around this camp. I checked into it."

"Then you have a very stupid commander."

"He said it doesn't matter anymore. The war's almost over."

"I think that he should at least see to it that a P.W. is painted on all the buildings! More importantly, who's the new prisoner?"

"We were just discussing that. Do you have any ideas?"

"Me?"

"They're holding him incommunicado."

"But you're the camp commander."

"The Waffen SS are holding him in strict isolation."

I asked Rolph, "How far away is the airport?"

"What airport?"

"They brought the new prisoner in by plane."

"They landed on the road at night. Pretty important, right?"

At breakfast I told Rolph, "I'd like to take a walk down to the highway."

"There's nothing to see down there and your fishing equipment should arrive any minute now. We've made arrangements with the Trout *Meister*."

"I still would like to walk down to the highway."

"That may be forbidden."

"But, you're not sure!"

Rolph shook his head.

I said, "Let's chance it."

"Us?"

"You're the camp commander."

"No!"

"Come on, what can happen? They'd just order us back. They won't shoot me."

"It's not you I'm worried about. I think they're looking for an excuse to shoot me. This SS of ours isn't one big happy family. The Waffen SS really don't appreciate the honorary SS They're beginning to blame us for losing the war."

I had to threaten Rolph before he agreed to accompany me. No one tried to stop us. Not even the troops manning the weapons carrier at the intersection leading to the guest house. The highway at that point ran straight and true for almost a mile. All of the telephone and power poles had been removed and the cables buried. It had been turned into a runway suitable for handling aircraft much larger than the Mosquito that I had arrived in. I asked Rolph, "When they brought the prisoner, did they happen to bring any baggage with him?" I was speculating about the kegs that held the fuel rods.

"No," said Rolph. "Just one man. There was a hood over his face."

I tried to sort it all out back in my room. *Who is it that they are so worried about escaping? But who would be foolish enough to try to escape with the war in its last hour.* I then thought, *Someone who didn't know? But they must have an inkling even in the worst of the concentration camps.*

Then I took another approach. The cell was protection. Protection from whom? Protection from the SS that weren't in on White Wash. Doubly secure not to contain its occupant, but to protect him. The occupant. Ah, hah, the occupant! Lily's big shot Nazi. The long time traitor to the cause on the verge of escaping with his neck with the consent of the OSS no matter what war crimes he had committed. The cover would be simple and allow him to disappear without a trace. A daring raid to rescue a well-known jurist and close friend of the late President from the clutches of the Gestapo. A raid that would go off without a hitch because the defenses of the guest house were so poor. A raid in which Rolph and every one of his men would be killed so that there would be no witnesses to the fact that there was more than one prisoner on the second floor.

It seemed like a foolish charade conceived at a Washington cocktail party by Ivy League graduates playing espionage agents. I thought of gathering Rolph's men in the dining room and explaining the facts of life to them. We would then break into the cell and hold our own little trial. An SS court of course, but what could be more fitting. Then I realized that the occupant of the cell may have been with us a long time, planted in the Nazi party or the Wehrmacht years before, and actually a hero of sorts.

The curiosity was driving me mad. He had to be an easily identifiable figure. I wasn't up on the Nazi hierarchy at that time, but I figured it to be one of three possibilities, Himmler, Goring, or Kaltenbrunner. Müller didn't seem important enough. I settled on Himmler, and then got the shock of my life.

## 44

Rolph burst into my room in a state of high excitement. He shouted, "Herr Colonel, the Führer is coming!"

"Who?" I asked sitting up.

"The Führer! He's coming to visit the camp. He's going to make his headquarters here."

I said, "You've got to be out of your mind."

"I was informed personally by General Müller. Until arrangements are made for his security, I'll have to ask you to remain in your room under guard."

Later, when I was dining in my room under the watchful eyes of a sleepy accountant from Munich Rolph entered with an embarrassed grin on his face. He released the guard and said, "It was just a joke."

"The Führer?"

"Müller has a bigger sense of humor than one would imagine. The Führer? No! Max Geisler! What's he doing here? This is for important prisoners. I mean, he was successful here in Bavaria, but internationally famous? Those Jews have all the connections... When he stepped out of the ambulance they brought him in, I almost saluted."

I told Rolph to close the door behind him and sit. As he did so he said, "I need a drink."

"Are you sure it was Max Geisler?"

"Of course! I worked with him years ago. He looks terrible now. They must have treated him horribly."

"Can I talk to him?"

"He went straight to bed."

"When Lily mentioned Geisler being in Munich, you were surprised. Why?" I asked.

"Anyone would have recognized him. I would have known about it."

"Right! He would have a hard time remaining incognito in the city."

"No really. There are a few Jews, well known Jews hiding out in Munich till this day. They have friends taking care of them. But—"

"But what?"

"Let me tell you, Herr Colonel, Max didn't have any friends. He was a bastard through and through. Everyone hated him. A textbook Jew. If you worked for him, you'd get paid in advance or you'd have to sue him to see one mark."

"He did impersonations of the Führer?"

"His Goring was better."

"When did they force him to stop?"

"Force him? He got the idea soon enough and started…" Rolph suddenly looked a bit uncomfortable.

I finished the sentence for him. "Playing up to the Nazis!"

Rolph nodded and then shrugged. "I have to admit I'm an opportunist. But Max, Max was an embarrassment to me. I worked with a lot of Jews. He was different, his nightclub act. He was their kind of Jew."

"Their kind?"

"The Party's. The anti-Semites. They're the ones that really thought he was funny."

"But he was a good actor?"

Maybe, but he never played anything but one character. The city slicker Jew."

"Except when he was impersonating Hitler?"

"And Goring and Goebbels."

"Rolph, I don't think Max was hiding out all these years. I think that he was happily employed as a double for Hitler."

"A double?"

"Political decoy. A substitute to throw people off. Churchill has at least one, Roosevelt probably did. Hitler's in one place, Max in another. Do you understand?"

A broad smile appeared on Rolph's face. "Max, the Jew? That would be a laugh." He ran his hand through his head of blond hair and then said, "Thinking about it, it's entirely possible. They're the same age, same build, same height. Come on, Herr Colonel. Max Geisler?"

I silently cursed Donavan, the OSS, and everyone else involved in operation "White Wash." Cursed them for conceiving it and cursed them for lowering themselves to deal with a demigod who started a World War that caused the death of millions and took my two sons from me. A man that turned a civilized people into a nation of raving maniacs, and then, when he realized that there was no way he could win, took command of his armed forces personally and sold them down the river in exchange for his own safety. A man the Allies never made an attempt to assassinate, because, as long as he lived, he was their shortest route to victory. A man that had to be convinced that things called Magnetic Fuel Rods had no real military value to deprive him of the secret weapon that he had long promised his followers. The Führer wasn't coming. He was here and so was Max. Yes, Adolph Hitler was less than three feet away from me, so cowardly in fact, that he was terrified of dwelling in anything less than a fortified bunker, and, yet, without remorse, would leave another to die in his place. Oh, yes, that's how it was going to happen. Hitler would be seen at the guest house, and then a lucky, Allied air strike, a rain of fire, a mutilated body, and a definitive end to the war.

Of course Hitler cooperates with a deal that lets him get away. But I couldn't let it happen. I would have to find a way to scuttle it. Roosevelt and Donovan had picked the wrong man for the job. But then I realized that I would have to decide if just punishment for Hitler was worth the life of even one G.I.? A life that would be saved by the war ending one day earlier, one moment earlier. The lives of thousands of our young men if the Magnetic Fuel Rods we got in exchange were of any use in the Pacific.

## 45

Judge Foster Binney thought, *And on top of it all, I had to outlive the whole bunch of them. This is my hell on earth. The protector of the Max Geislers, the guardian of Crowell Collier, the champion of a nation's self-respect. God damn that woman! God damn Simon Blake! The secret has to be kept. There's no other way.*

He dialed the number engraved on his pocket watch and said into the telephone, "Control? ... This is Colonel Binney! ... The remaining Max Geisler is in extreme jeopardy. You must immediately, I repeat, immediately, execute three men. Their names and addresses are as follows... The first is Simon Blake." As Binney read off the list, he cried.

## 46

Simon woke before dawn and looked at Jane Scott sleeping at his side, her face turned away. The evening before had gone badly. They had dinner with the Hollywood writer working on the Crowell script with her and his eighteen-year-old actress girlfriend. The man was at least five years older than Simon, clad in jeans, and an unbuttoned, silk shirt. He had an obvious hair transplant. Simon couldn't get a word in edgewise. Simon listened dutifully and, when there was a gap in the conversation, asked, "Do you use Grecian Formula on your chest?"

To top it all off, when they left the restaurant, an old man bumped into Simon on the street and poked him rudely with his umbrella. Simon would have punched him if it weren't for Jane.

He dressed silently, kissed Jane on the cheek, and started home hoping to slip into his own bed before Gilda woke up. It was on the West side Highway that he noticed a Green Chevy Impala with two men inside was following him. He exited at 125th Street and drove back downtown again just to make sure. When he checked his rearview mirror on Broadway, the Chevy was still in sight. His first thought was that Gilda had gotten wind of his affair with Jane and had hired private detectives to get the goods on him. *That absolutely couldn't be! She never showed the least bit interest in what I did before. But who the hell knows what goes on in her mind?*

He continued on downtown to West 83rd Street and stopped in front of the building and looked back over his shoulder. As the Impala turned the corner, Simon stepped on the gas and with a screeching start made the left on to Riverside Drive jumping the light, a left on West 82nd Street, and the right on to West End Avenue thinking, "If those bastards want to snoop, I'll give them the ride of their lives."

Simon sped all the way down to 46th Street and then turned towards the highway again. As he went up the ramp he held the accelerator down until the speedometer read 90 miles an hour. The distance between him and the Chevy was growing too great for sport. He didn't want to lose them that easily. He thought, "Now, the scare of their lives."

Simon reached over, opened his brief case, and removed the package containing the Luger and undid it as he slowed down to allow the Impala to catch up with him. As it drew closer, Simon slowed even more. He planned to cut the Chevy off, shove the Luger into the face of the driver and order him to explain why he was tailing him. The Impala picked up speed, and much to Simon's surprise, tried to cut him off. "Robbery!" flashed through Simon's mind as he deftly maneuvered the Cadillac onto the shoulder of the road and stepped on the gas to pull alongside of the Chevy and lower the window of the Seville intending to scare off the occupants of the other car. Instead, he heard the burst of gunfire that punctured the rear door of the Seville with bullet holes.

"Fucking bastards!" screamed Simon. "Kidnappers!" Taking both hands off the wheel, he slipped a clip into the Luger and cocked it. That's it, he thought. *Play dead and get those bastards close enough to blast them. No—get good cover!*

*Pretend you're in your old Sherman.* He thought of Morris's words of long ago. "Don't go chasing after the krauts in that tank of yours. Pick your ground and force them to fight on your terms."

"Just who do they think they're fucking with," shouted Simon. "I'm not afraid. I've been shot at before." Organizing his thoughts quickly, he decided that the low hills, twisting driveways, and high hedges of his own neighborhood would be perfect to ambush the Chevy. He just as quickly discarded the idea. He didn't want to bring the fight home to a residential area. There was his family, the neighbors' kids. He needed a safe place, no civilians, a place that he knew like the back of his hand. "This is my fucking tank, baby," he thought as he shouted orders at an imaginary driver and gunner below him. Under his thumbs, the leather covered wheel of the Seville became the twin butterfly triggers of a .50 caliber machine gun. A truck was behind him, blinking his lights to pass. Simon slowed down to let it by, cringing ever so slightly in case it was the enemy also. It wasn't and he couldn't see the Chevy. Simon got into the lane behind the truck to use it as a shield, his armor plate, in case trouble lay ahead. "Know your own ground! The shopping center! I planned it. I practically built it with my own hands! Flat as a virgin's tummy. Good tank country, baby! The Bower Memorial Mall, baby! They told me it was a lousy name for a shopping center and I told them to shut the fuck up. I named it after a kid I knew that got his in Normandy."

The red brake lights ahead of him blinked on and off and the truck started to slow down. Simon pulled over to the left to see what was ahead. A white, Dodge Dart blocked two lanes as if it had been in an accident. A man of about Simon's age, holding a flash light, directed the truck through a tight squeeze on the right. "Those bastards have more than one car and a radio! If I'm wrong I'm a schmuck, but not dead. If I'm right, I'm still not dead."

Simon swung back into the right lane. Just as the truck was about to come abreast of the Dodge, he drove onto the shoulder of the road using the larger vehicle to cover his left flank and, at the same time, looking for another ambush position. A roadside clump of bushes seemed likely. Someone could lay flat behind them and fire into the Seville's right side. Simon drove the gas pedal to the floor and aimed straight for the foliage. A man there, armed with a shotgun, looked up in surprise just as the fender of the Seville smashed into his head. Simon slammed on his brakes, shifted into reverse, and backed over the corpse for good measure.

Simon had slipped back in time and began to think that he was actually driving a Sherman. He reached down for the lever to reverse the direction of his right tread to spin the tank around and grind the body into the earth just as a third man rolled out of the wrong side of the Chevy with a submachine gun. Simon threw the Seville into drive and raced away before his new opponent could aim.

As he pulled away, Simon reached into his jacket pocket for a cigar, lit it, and thought, *One thing that I always thought ridiculous would certainly come in handy now. A C.B.! My God damn tank had a radio! I could call for help.* He let out a whoop and shouted into the wind, "Who the hell needs any help. I've been through all this before."

The distance between him and the Dodge and the Chevy was growing but he didn't want the fight to break off that soon. He eased off on the gas pedal so that they wouldn't lose him completely and thought, "Who—

Binney? The Nazis? It doesn't matter! Winning matters!" He began to plan, assuming that there were other cars with radios.

"What will the next one try to do? Ram me? That's it... Ram!" Simon kept just enough ahead of the cars following to render their weapons useless and concentrated on his right.

A New York City taxicab moving towards the highway on the service road tried to keep parallel with Simon's car. The taxi adjusted its speed to bisect his line of travel. Simon slammed on the power brakes and swung the wheel over to put the heavy car into a tire burning spin just as the driver of the cab gave it all it had in an attempt to sideswipe the Seville. The cab missed him by less than an inch, hitting the divider at an oblique angle, flipping over, rear wheels first, and landing on its roof with enough momentum for it to careen off the far side of the highway. Simon slowed down again. Traffic was picking up and he didn't want his pursuers to lose him.

The additional traffic offered another element of danger. If his antagonists had more cars, he would have to be a near genius to pick them out from the civilians on the road. Then one, further ahead, in the right lane, played its hand too early. It was forcing all the cars behind him to pass. "That's a baddie!" shouted Simon. "He's going to blast me as I pass him." The car, a small Mazda, pulled over into the left lane as Simon caught up with it. Simon fell behind and slightly to the right of the import.

He saw the weapon a moment later when the man next to the driver leaned out of the window to fire. Simon stepped on the gas and steered to the left, squeezing between the Mazda and the divider so that his wheels rode on the concrete like a skateboard. Letting the other car and the divider keep the Cadillac in line, Simon raised the Luger, steadied it with both hands, and shot the driver of the Mazda in the left temple. As the small car began to wobble erratically, Simon stepped on the gas while the man seated next to the driver in the Mazda managed to break, pull the driver from the seat, start up the vehicle, and continue the chase.

Simon took the George Washington Bridge and each subsequent turn as fast as the Seville could handle it but not fast enough to get too far ahead of his new enemies. He wondered why the cars chasing him weren't specifically souped-up for the kind of business they were engaged in and then he slowed down and put on his turn signal as he approached the mall so the chase cars knew where he was going. Hitting the brakes at the stop sign at the bottom of the ramp, he again waited for his pursuers before making the left and sharp right into the mall's deserted parking lot. Simon drove up onto the pedestrian walkway and stopped until he was sure that the other cars were still after him. He then drove through a covered arcade, making a left smashing through the window of a Mercedes dealer's office, and a right through a flimsy office wall where he cut off the engine. He had good cover and an excellent field of fire through the front window of the dealership which faced the plaza.

Simon hoped that none of his pursuers were in armor during the war. He was using a very old trick. He estimated that he had about fifteen minutes before the silent alarm in the dealership would bring private security people and the local cops. He didn't need any help.

**47**

There was a light rain at six forty-five in the morning as Parri waited under the awning of the Taft Hotel. When he saw Ray in the rear of a yellow cab, he leaped forward, flung open the door, and jumped in the back. "Please," he said. "Tell the driver to keep on going, Mr. Warren. I have to talk to you."

"Who the hell are you?" asked Ray.

"I work for Judge Binney. Remember? I have to talk to you. It's important."

"What's wrong with the hotel?"

"I don't think it's safe."

"Shoot!"

"I've been trying to reach you in Washington all night. I checked the hotel again and they told me you had a reservation."

Ray paid off the taxi on 58th Street and 7th Avenue. As they sat in an all-night coffee shop, Ray said, "Okay, no one's listening. What was wrong with the hotel?"

"There may be someone waiting there to kill you."

"Who?"

"I don't know. The Judge started acting strange yesterday afternoon. And I mean strange. Senile! He's been muttering all night, I murdered Blake and the others. I shouldn't have called Control."

"Control?"

"Don't ask me," said Parri. "Control. That's what he said."

"What do you think Control is?"

"I haven't the slightest idea, Mr. Warren. I've been with the Judge twenty-four hours a day for the last year. I mean everybody he's been in touch with is on the up and up. He never tried to hide from me or his secretary."

"Never?"

Parri exhaled through his teeth. "Not until yesterday. He made a call from a telephone booth and asked me to leave him be for about ten minutes. And, after he got the letter from Germany, he sent me out of the room. I think he made a call."

"What letter?"

"It was an ad about the building that Mr. Blake put in the German papers."

"Mr. Blake? .... Then why does he want to kill me?"

"You and Mr. Blake. He said you both should have minded your business."

"Simon—Jesus Christ!" Ray leaped up and ran to the telephone. He dialed Simon's house and waited impatiently until Gilda answered.

"Goddam let me speak to Simon."

"I don't think he came home last night. Is there anything wrong?"

"No, just some important business."

Ray next called Jane Scott. He asked. "Is Simon there?"

"He left."

"How long ago?"

"About an hour or two. I was dead asleep."

"Were you with him all night?"

"Since cocktails!" said Jane. "What's up?"

"Did anything unusual happen?"

"He was awfully insulting to some of my friends."

"That's not unusual. Did he run into any strangers?"

"Strangers? Yeah, some old man bumped into him. Is that what you mean?"

"What happened then?"

"The old man poked Simon with his umbrella."

Ray cursed under breath and then asked her, "And?"

"Simon looked like he was going to punch the geezer, but I cooled him down."

"Jane, how did he feel?"

"Who?"

"Simon!" say Ray anxiously. "Afterwards!"

"Simon was in great shape. Why?"

"If you hear from him tell him to call me immediately at his house."

"His house?"

"I'll be there." Ray hung up and then called Braddock at home in Virginia and told him to fly to New York with a company toxicologist. He gave him Simon's address.

## 48

The three cars pulled up in the pedestrian plaza and seven unexceptional looking, middle-aged men got out. Three of them were armed with M-1 submachine guns with wire stocks and bulky, old fashioned silencers. An eight year old, white Ford van appeared on the southern pedestrian walkway and bounced down the steps onto the plaza and stopped. The old man who had tangled with Simon the night before got out of the back of the van and crossed to the others. Simon turned the Seville's ignition key slowly and then backed up to clear the Mercedes in front of him, whispering to himself, "Sorry fellows, but this is what you get for bunching up in combat."

As he eased the automatic shift lever into third, the group broke apart and headed back to their respective vehicles, leaving the old man and a bald, chubby cheeked fellow in heated conversation. As the cars and the van sped off in four different directions, Simon stepped on the gas, and careening through the window wall of the auto dealership, aimed directly for the two remaining men.

Age had taken away their agility. The chubby fellow flew up into the air landing about seven feet ahead of the Seville with a sickening splat. Simon's left front wheel crushed his chest as he attempted to rise again.

As his car bounced over the body, Simon turned sharply to the right. The old man was on his knees attempting to cock the .45 automatic he held. Simon flung open the car door, kicked the pistol out of his grasp, and grabbed him by the collar of his long, black raincoat. Jamming the Luger into his head, Simon demanded, "What's all this about, hey?" The old man dug his boney fingers into Simon's wrist in an attempt to break loose as the Chevy came into sight and headed directly towards the Seville.

One of the men inside leaped out and fired. The last round in his clip struck the old man who exhaled with a woosh as if he had been kicked the chest. Simon flung the body away and slid back behind the wheel, his foot hitting the gas pedal before his behind touched the seat. With a shriek of burning rubber he bounced the Cadillac up the steps of the plaza and on to the easternmost walkway knocking over a fast film kiosk as he did so.

The Chevy didn't follow. A thinnish fellow in a gray, single breasted suit, wearing eye glasses, leaned over the old man and fired a round into his head to make sure that he was dead. Simon decided that it was time to stop playing games and head for the State Police barracks for help, but, when he drove towards the exit he found it effectively blocked by the Dodge Dart which had stationed itself lengthwise between a shoe store and a pet shop. The passengers took up positions behind the vehicle. The Chevy was bouncing up the steps to blockade the other end of the pedestrian arcade.

Simon threw the Seville into reverse, backed up until he came abreast of the "Home Deco Center," swung the wheel all the way to the right, crashed through its picture windows, and squeezed between rows of counters on both sides until he came to an escalator, where he turned left plowing through a stacked glassware display, and then right, two aisles down, where he smashed through a wall separating the selling area from a store room.

When he reached the store's loading ramp, he leaped out of the car, and pressed the "up" button of the freight elevator's overhead door. As it rose slowly, Simon ran back to the Seville, put it into drive, and started forward. The Dodge came into sight and blocked the ramp leading to the loading dock just as the Chevy came through the plasterboard wall. Simon shifted into reverse, slammed into the left rear door of the Chevy, knocking its occupants sprawling, went into drive, and turned right scraping against a concrete pillar. He stepped on the brakes, swung the wheel over, spun around, and without coming to a full stop, drove into the freight elevator where he leaped out of the driver's seat, yanked down the overhead door, and pushed the down button. When the car descended to the basement level, Simon drove into the service area that separated "The Home Deco Center" from a fast food restaurant. He smashed through another plasterboard wall and into the paint department. Simon got out of the car, tossed a half dozen cans of paint remover into the back seat of the Seville, heard running feet, and dived behind a display case just as one of the men came to the head of the wide stairs leading down to the basement, and fired at him. He was pinned down and the range was too great for him to return the fire. A second burst hit a row of cans above his head and splattered Simon with vinyl paint.

A security guard with a drawn pistol appeared out of nowhere shouted to the man on the balcony, "Freeze!" The man swung around and cut the security guard in half with a long burst from his weapon. When he looked back down again, Simon was gone. The man cursed and slipping a new clip into the submachine gun, threw a few rounds into the roof of the Seville in frustration.

Simon hugged the wall below his antagonist trying to divine his next move. The man started down the steps cautiously. Simon moved a stepladder on display to the underside of the staircase, climbed it silently, and looked between the metal rungs of the stairs. A pair of bulky space shoes came into sight. Simon raised the Luger and, just as the man shifted his weight to take another step, fired a single bullet into his right ankle. The man did a complete somersault, breaking his collarbone as he landed on the edge of a metal step. He slid the rest of the way down, the M-1 submachine gun bouncing ahead of him. Simon leaped off the ladder, ran forward, and fired a single shot into the man's brain. He then retrieved the submachine gun and began to go through the man's pockets as the white Ford van crashed through the exterior window wall of the deco center. Two men got out it and ran towards the balcony to meet a burst from the submachine gun in Simon's hands.

As they dived for cover, Simon ran back to the Seville, fired another burst at the balcony to keep them down, put the car into drive, and drove through another plasterboard wall into a Bloomingdale's stock room. Backing up and shifting down to get enough power to get past a stubborn showcase, he then sped forward mowing down a row of mannequins. He hit the brakes at the Gucci counter, grabbed a handful of silk scarves, dropped them into his lap, and stepped on the gas to smash through the far wall knocking down a display of expensive audio components and a rack of color television portables on the opposite side. He drove forward through a line of television consoles, rack after rack of records and tapes, and finally two displays of hard cover books before turning sharply to avoid a pillar and left to break through another window wall that led him into an employees' underground parking area where he pulled the car up behind a ramp for cover.

He uncapped the cans of kerosene and paint remover and stuffed the Gucci silks into them to serve as wicks. Before starting the Seville again, he checked his solid gold Dunhill lighter to make sure it was still working. He estimated that he had at least seven more men and three soft skinned vehicles to contend with. The numbers were important. He had to take at least one man alive and find out what the hell was going on. No one had raised as much as a finger against him since his last fire fight in Steinhoffen.

Simon drove up to the plaza level exit of the underground garage noticing for the first time that his left cheek and shoulder were covered with blood and peppered with multiple glass fragments. At the top of the ramp, he got out of the Seville, crawled forward, pressed the up button of the overhead door, and then ran back to the car. He gunned the Seville up the exit ramp and bounced out onto the pavement of the parking lot where he came to a dead stop fifty feet from the corner of the building.

He left the car and crawled forward to look around the corner. The Dodge Dart was parked by a loading dock. Simon crawled back to his car, got a can of paint remover, tipped it to moisten the wick, and then fired the last three rounds in the submachine gun to give away his position before running forward to the corner of the building and throwing himself flat against the ground.

Simon lit the Gucci scarves and as the Dart came abreast of him, flung the flaming can into the driver's side window. The driver swerved to the right instinctively as the can exploded roasting the interior of the compact. A screaming, blazing figure fell out of the right hand door. Simon ran back to the Seville, put it into reverse, backed up, and then drove down the steps onto the plaza where he caught sight of the Mazda in the western walkway moving slowly away from him. Aiming directly for it, he stepped on the gas, drove across the plaza, up onto the walkway, and smashed into its rear end driving the smaller car into the window of a bakery. Simon hit the brakes, backed up, and then rocketed forward into the Mazda once more, catching the driver half out of the front door. A glass pastry rack in the window of the bakery had decapitated the Mazda's other occupant. Looking back towards the plaza, Simon saw the Chevy emerge from the eastern walkway and head across the plaza towards him. He backed the Seville up to the far end of the covered arcade, lit the scarves in the remaining cans of paint remover, stepped on the gas, and hit the cruise control. He then rolled over into the back seat and out the back door, taking cover behind a litter basket.

The Chevy slowed down, turned to the right to block the Seville's exit, and stopped. It occupants leaped out to the side and began firing at the Cadillac as it nosed into the Chevy with a dull crunch. Simon had set the fuse a little too long. The men were already peering in the window when the five cans exploded into a fireball that engulfed them. Simon's next target was the van, but he found it exceedingly hard to rise from the pavement of the arcade. When he finally got to his knees, he realized that he was having trouble breathing. He gasped, "Medic!" before collapsing.

## 49

The driver of the white Ford van was trying to decide if he should drive towards the sound of the last explosion or remain in place as ordered. Before he was able to make that decision, dozens of police cars converged on the mall. The driver put the van into gear, and following the exit signs, decided to break off contact for the day. As he turned onto the service road and headed for Route 4, two State Police cars cut off both lanes in front of him. The van made a tight U-turn, only to discover three more police cars, with lights flashing and sirens blaring, approaching from the south. The driver sighed, stopped the van, turned off the ignition, and lit a cigarette. He waited until he was surrounded by police vehicles. He then calmly picked up a pistol from the seat next to him, cocked it, placed the barrel in his mouth, and fired. The area suddenly fell silent. Two young State Police troopers approached the van cautiously as a voice on a loud hailer behind them ordered the occupants to come out with their hands up.

One of the troopers tried the handle of the van's rear door. Finding it unlocked, he turned it and swung the door open wide. The trooper backing him up aimed his shotgun inside and shouted, "Freeze!"

An elderly gentleman in a red flannel shirt, jeans, and seated in a wheel chair removed a set of earphones from his head, smiled, said, "Hi!" and then took a hand grenade from under the blanket on his lap. He pulled out the pin, and whirling about suddenly, bent over to cushion the blast with his own body so that none of the State Troopers would be wiped out.

# 50

Ray barged past a police guard into the Intensive Care Unit where they were treating Simon and demanded that he be given toxicological tests immediately. The Doctor on duty tried to assure him that Simon was suffering from a heart attack and nothing more. A tall, lanky State Police Sergeant broke up the argument and began to question Ray who felt it best to play dumb until he learned the full extent of the battle at the shopping center. He then called Langley and told them to pass the information along to Braddock who was on his way to New York.

He then called Simon's son-in-law and asked him to track down Morris and Sam. A nurse came up to Ray and said, "Mr. Blake would like to talk to you before he sees his family."

Ray followed her back into the I.C.U. Simon looked up at Ray and said, "This isn't the first time I've had an attack, but Gilda doesn't know."

Ray leaned over and whispered, "It may not have been a heart attack."

"No, buddy! The same as last time, only worse."

Ray whispered, "That was some job at the shopping center."

"Shit," said Simon. "They were only soft skinned vehicles."

Ray whispered, "You weren't in an M-Four. What really happened?"

"You tell me what happened."

"The Judge!"

"He had to be with those old farts! They should have stayed in their rocking chairs instead of fooling with an armored cavalry vet."

"As far as you're concerned, it was a kidnapping attempt. That's a direct order."

The State Police Sergeant entered the room with two doctors. One of them looked at Simon and then Ray before asking, "Who came up with this thing about poison?"

Ray replied, "I believe that the kidnappers tried to neutralize Mr. Blake with an exotic substance."

"Really? Who are you?"

"A friend of the family!"

The State Police Sergeant said, "Mr. Warren comes highly recommended by the F.B.I."

"Well, Mr. Warren, I'm the Chief of Pathology here. We're running additional tests on your friend's blood, but as far as we're concerned it's nothing but a coronary. To ease your mind, we'll go further. How do you think this substance was administered?"

"By injection."

"We'll take a look," said the pathologist.

By the time Braddock's helicopter settled on the hospital's landing pad, the pathologist had asked Ray down to his office where he showed him a microscopic silver dart. He said, "At first I thought you were out of your mind, but I found this in his buttock. It's filled with a substance I haven't as yet identified."

"What's taking you so long?"

"It's harmless! Whatever it was loaded with is still in there. It didn't dissolve into his blood stream if that's what it was supposed to do."

The incident at the shopping center was released to the press as an aborted kidnapping and toned down completely. Braddock set up an unofficial office in a motel near Simon's home. When Ray reported there, Braddock said, "Your friend Simon is someone for the books."

"A guy on the radio said he should run for President."

"That's the best idea I've heard all day. Our current one will hand him the job. I laid things out for him and he did our theory one better without any prompting. He thinks, What if our Armandas and Rockefellers were so worried about the Communists that they helped fund the Nazi Party? If he fell for our little stunt, so will the Russians. He gave me carte blanche an hour ago."

"Let's get to work on Binney. And, may I add, by any means."

"The President has already spoken to him. Binney told him that the whole shopping center thing sounded ridiculous and if he continues to pester him about it, he'll go to the press."

"We're going to have to lean on that old bastard."

"No way! The old coot is too smart for us. He conveniently had a stroke after he hung up on the President. He's closeted in a hospital. The report is that if he recovers at all, it'll be without the power of speech. I wonder how long he's been rehearsing that bit?"

"Any I.D. on the K.I.A.s?"

"You figure?" said Braddock. "They're from all parts of the country. Average Americans, if you want to call them that. Their friends and families haven't the slightest idea what they were doing in New Jersey with machine guns. Oh, yes, they had one thing in common. They were all World War Two veterans."

"They were part of an organization!"

"Of course, they were part of an organization. The OSS!"

"Oh, wow!" said Ray.

"I don't have to tell you what the President feels about having a secret organization running around loose in the United States, especially one that thinks it's part of the U.S. government. Incidentally, you were right. They tried to terminate your friend with a dart last night. It was made for the OSS in Nineteen Forty Five. It only had a shelf life of five years. When it didn't work, our friends panicked and hit Blake with everything they had."

"Let's hope Simon simplified things by knocking them all off."

"He didn't. After I heard the extent of the business at the shopping center, I had your home and the hotel staked out. There's two over-aged assassins waiting for you in the lobby of the Taft, and the F.B.I. found another duo in your apartment. They started shooting as soon as the front door was opened. The instant they realized it wasn't you, but Federal Agents, one shot himself in the head, and the other jumped out of the window."

"Shit! Do you have a drink?" asked Ray.

"There's those little bottles in the refrigerator. They charge a fortune for them."

"Put it on the expense account. I deserve it. The next thing you're going to tell me is that I have to turn up at the Taft tomorrow."

"Tonight, at twenty four hundred hours. We want to see if they have a second shift."

Ray flipped open the refrigerator door and grabbed the first bottle in sight. As he unscrewed the cap, he said, "God damn that lousy building, it's a curse, and—"

"And what?" asked Braddock.

"It's a blessing. I didn't fly in this morning. I took a plane yesterday afternoon. I met a woman in Three Eighty Nine while I was working on this matter. I promised her dinner. I ended up spending the night with her. If it weren't for her and the building, I would have been home. I may have not been as alert as Simon."

They dressed Ray in armored underwear strong enough to stop a high-powered bullet. He was also equipped with a suit bag lined with two layers of armored cloth on top of a thick foam pad, which, if the need arose, could be used as a shield to cover his face and head. Before he got into a cab driven by an F.B.I. agent, he asked Braddock, "What do these guys look like?"

"Senior citizens. Try not to hurt them."

"Try not to hurt them?"

"The first team backing you up will be armed with tranquilizer guns. There will be others with heavier stuff, but only if it's really necessary. We need one alive. The odds are that he'll talk."

"How will they recognize me?" asked Ray.

"They've been calling the desk periodically asking if you've checked in yet. When you go to the desk, the clerk will tell you that your room isn't ready yet. You'll go to the coffee shop. You'll be paged five minutes later. That should do the trick. The desk clerk's an F.B.I. agent as well as most of the other front office people."

When the taxi pulled up in front of the Taft, the doorman greeted Ray with a loud, "Hello, Mr. Warren." Ray carried his own luggage up to the desk and asked for the room he had reserved. As per plan, the clerk told him that it wasn't ready yet. He would be paged. Ray bought a copy of *The New York Times* and waited in the coffee shop until they called his name.

As he returned to the lobby, a potbellied man in a bowling jacket rose and followed him. After he registered at the desk, the same man was waiting with a slim, expensively tailored companion of the same age. Two F.B.I types hurried up and entered the elevator ahead of them. Ray figured that they were good guys because they were both in their early thirties. A woman also got into the car.

Ray asked for his floor wondering why the older men were taking so long to act. He purposely backed into the fat man and brushed his belly with his elbow. It was enough to tell him that he had at least ten sticks of dynamite strapped around his waist.

As they followed him out of the car on his floor, Ray swung around and hit the heavy man with the metal covered edge of his attaché case, stunning him. As Ray hit him a second time, the older man in the expensive clothes lunged at him holding a thin, sharp knife. The blade skidded off the armored vest as two tranquilizer darts bit into the assailant's back.

They began to take effect almost immediately and the man in the suit buckled at the knees. With one great effort, he threw himself upon his heavyset companion and embraced him, reaching under his bowling jacket at the same time. Ray screamed, "Dynamite!" and shoved the two young F.B.I. agents back into the elevator and made it in with them. The door slid shut a moment before the charge wrapped around the fat man's waist went off.

It took the Emergency Squad and the Fire Department more than an hour to remove the door of the elevator which was warped just enough to keep the car from moving. No one inside was seriously hurt. The car's thick steel walls and the masonry of its shaft shielded the occupants from the full force of the explosion.

## 51

As Ray nursed a wrenched back in a hot tub, there was a knock at the door of his hotel room. He yelled, "Just a minute," and then, wrapping a towel around his waist, asked cautiously, "Yes?"

"The bell boy. You left your bag downstairs."

"Okay!" said Ray. He opened the door a crack and peered out. A stooped, old, uniformed bellboy stood waiting patiently with Ray's overnighter. Ray slipped the chain off the door, opened it. As he turned to get his billfold for a tip, a metallic tube filled with cyanide gas appeared in the wizened bellboy's hand. Ray jumped back with a shout, reaching wildly for something to hit with, as the bellboy pressed forward trying to get close enough to release the gas in Ray's face.

The doors leading to a connecting suite and the hall burst open. Braddock and a half dozen Federal agents rushed into the room. They pinned the bellboy to the floor, separating him from his weapon at the same time.

One of the agents forced the bellboy's mouth open and inserted a wedge between his teeth to keep him from biting down. As another agent searched his mouth for a capsule, a third injected him with a hypodermic syringe. Quickly stripping him of all his clothes, they manacled his legs and wrapped him in a straitjacket.

He carried no identification. The only thing in his pockets was an "L" pill which he never got the opportunity to use. When the effects of the tranquilizer wore off, the prisoner asked for coffee and a Danish pastry and then said, "You didn't have to be that rough. I had no plans to use the suicide pill. That was part of the game I wasn't going to play."

"Game?" asked one of the agents. "Attempted murder."

"Murder? I'm a member of the U.S. Armed Forces carrying out orders."

"The Armed Forces?"

"The Office of Strategic Services."

"Who gave you orders to kill Mr. Warren?"

"My headquarters," replied the bellboy.

"Your headquarters?" said the agent. "And where may that be?"

The bellboy shrugged. "I don't know. They called me and had the proper code words, Lodge Pole. It was the first time. In all these years they never called before."

"Who are you?" asked another agent.

"Harbour! Joe Harbour. Master Sergeant Joe Harbour, U.S. Army Reserve. I'm a retired Maryland State Police officer. Same business as you people, almost. How about that? They finally called me. Those guys from Control. Is this an exercise?"

"How did they find you? You didn't keep the same address all these years?"

"We were ordered to put an ad in *The New York Times*. You know, Karen baby, your Uncle Jake misses you. My team was Uncle Jake. I never thought they'd call. They paid us every month so we played along. When I got the word yesterday I figured, what the hell, I'm obligated. It was more like bored. What the hell, it's all for the good of the country, isn't it?"

"Is what?" asked an agent.

"This business. Don't you know what it's about? They never told us. They just gave my team a lot of training and supplied us with weapons. Then they told us to get lost until Control called. Like I said, thirty-five years later and here I am. Can you tell me what it's all about?"

Braddock entered the room. He said sharply, "I think you know a lot more than you're admitting."

"If you don't know what it's all about, why did you try to stop me? I mean, you should have nabbed one of the guys in surveillance or communications. Not my group. My group was a combat team."

Braddock sat next to the man and asked, "Your group? The guys that blew themselves up in the hall?"

"Those guys? No way! My guys were all combat vets. The guys in the hall were from surveillance and communications."

"Where's the rest of your group now?" asked an agent.

The man shook his head sadly. "We used to train together every other weekend. Three of us that is. Pete Washington, he was in the Marine Reserve and got called up for Korea. He got it on the reservoir .... Then there was a polish guy, Marty. A paratrooper. Real nice guy, never said a word. Went fishing by himself one day. Drowned .... Then there was big Carl. Lung cancer! When I got the call from Control I told them that it was only me left. They said they knew, but it was a go anyway. I went down to the cellar, dug up the artillery, and drove to New York. Those other two weirdoes, that would have never happened if I had Marty, Pete, and Big Carl with me. I knew they didn't have it in them when I met them yesterday. That's why we split up." He hesitated and then said, "Tell them that I tried. Tell them I kept my weapons in good shape. I turned those dynamite sticks every week for thirty five years like clockwork."

"Tell who?" asked Braddock.

"The guys in Control."

"Did you know Foster Binney in the service?" asked Braddock. "A Colonel Foster Binney?"

"No, I never heard that name."

"Who recruited you into the OSS?" asked Braddock.

"A Colonel. I was an M.P. at that time. A Colonel? Let's see .... Yeah, Colonel Champion. Jack Champion."

The F.B.I. agents looked at Braddock. He said, "I know who you mean. He passed away about twenty years ago."

## 52

They moved Ray to a large suite and placed heavily armed agents in both the bedroom and living room. He slept soundly until the telephone rang about two o'clock in the morning. The agent in the bedroom shook Ray awake and handed him the phone. Braddock said, "I hate to do this to you, but something important's come up."

"What have you got?" asked Ray.

"It's your friend Morris. I'm dreadfully sorry, Ray, but we had no idea he was on the hit list or we would have done something sooner."

Morris Ankhorn was in Roosevelt Hospital with multiple stab wounds. A surgical resident told Ray, "He's not going to make it. I've seen worse, but he's not going to make it. He's on in years and hasn't taken care of himself. On top of everything else his liver is enlarged and he has a high blood sugar count."

"Can I see him?" asked Ray. The resident nodded and showed him in.

Ray leaned over the bed and said softly, "Captain?"

It took some time for Morris to become aware of Ray's presence. When his eyes finally turned to the left and looked up they filled with recognition. A tear formed in one of them. He tried to speak.

Ray said, "Take it easy, Captain. We'll talk tomorrow."

Morris shook his head, raised his hand, and motioned Ray closer.

Ray put his ear to Morris's lips and took his hand and squeezed it.

Morris gasped, "Tell Simon I'm sorry. I apologize. Don't forget to tell Simon I ...."

"Come on Captain, you don't have to apologize. For what? Take care of yourself and we'll go out and get blasted just like old times."

"I apologize!" Tears streamed from Morris's eyes.

"For what?" asked Ray, trying to smile.

"Apologize ...."

"Come on Captain, there's nothing to apologize for."

Morris tried to sit up.

"Please!" said Ray.

"Apologize ...."

"For what?"

"Steinhoffen ...."

"Steinhoffen?" asked Ray.

"And the building ...." Morris's head fell back against the pillow and his mouth hung open in death.

## 53

Parri cried himself to sleep at night. He had become so attached to the Judge that watching the old man change dramatically from a vigorous, sharp-witted bon vivant to a shriveled, aged, recluse in a matter of moments was too much for him. Binney had to be dressed and undressed, lifted into his wheel chair every morning, every night, and every time one of his bodily functions called. He had lost the power of speech. Parri read *The New York Times* to him every morning. The Judge would motion him closer when a particular article interested him and motion for it to be repeated over and over again.

After he had been out of the hospital for a month, the Judge took fifteen minutes to communicate to Parri that he wished to be dressed in a business suit and then be driven to the office. He then laboriously wrote out a telephone number on a scrap of paper, handed it to Parri, and took another fifteen minutes to explain that he wanted the number called at nine fifteen sharp. Parri was to tell a Mr. Smith that the Judge wasn't able to keep a previous luncheon appointment.

When the Judge's limousine pulled up outside the law offices of Cabot, Stiles, Rothschild, and Binney, it took him twenty minutes to ask Parri to run ahead and take care of his mail as he had some gift shopping to do.

Parri tried to talk the Judge out of the idea, but finally relented with the thought that the excursion would be good for the old man.

When Parri was out of sight, the Judge handed his chauffeur a note he had written earlier directing him to drive to the Macy's in Queens. When they arrived at the department store, Binney handed the chauffeur a shopping list and five, one hundred dollar bills. The chauffeur glanced at the list and then said, "This is going to take me some time, sir. It's all over the store. You sure you don't want me to put you into the chair and take you along? That's better than sitting here all alone in the car." Binney shook his head vigorously.

The Judge waited until the chauffeur had been gone for ten minutes before he removed a fresh cigar from his pocket, lit it, and took a deep puff. He then put on his gloves and got out of the car. Walking at a brisk pace, he dodged traffic, crossing Queens Boulevard against the light. On the opposite side, he turned right, checking the street signs until he found the one he wanted, turned left, and hurried down a quiet shopping street until he found the cross street he was looking for, one lined with single family homes. He turned right again, discovered that the numbers were too high for the address he was seeking, reversed his direction, and kept on going until he came upon a simple, brick faced, frame residence set a little back from the street. Without breaking stride he walked up to the door and rang the bell. A few moments later, a gray haired woman in her fifties appeared, opened the door wide and asked, "Yes?"

"Is your husband at home?"

"My husband?"

"Mr. Sullivan!" said the Judge impatiently.

"He's not my husband," replied the woman.

"Oh?" said the Judge.

"I work for him. His mail order business."

"Is he in?"

"Of course," said the woman. "But—"

"I'm an old friend of his. A very old friend. Colonel Binney. Foster Binney."

The woman led Binney to a small, cramped living room, and then went upstairs. She returned in a few minutes and said, "He's just getting up. Do you want some coffee?"

"Yes," said Binney.

When she returned with coffee, he asked, "Have you worked for Mr. Sullivan long?"

"Oh, my God, yes! Nearly thirty five years."

"He must have been in the army when you started?"

"Just afterwards," said the woman.

"Were you in the army?" asked the Judge.

"Me?" said the woman. "What makes you ask that?"

"I remember seeing you in Washington."

"She's never been to Washington," said Sullivan from the top of the stairs. He was about twenty years younger than the Judge and his close cropped gray hair made him look even younger. As he came down into the living room, he said, "What can I do for you, Colonel?"

"I'm Foster Binney."

"The name doesn't ring a bell."

"You're in the mail order business, aren't you?"

"Stamps and coins. Just an extension of a hobby of mine."

"Really? I must have the wrong Sullivan."

"There are lots of Sullivans. Come into the office. Just stamps and coins. See for yourself."

Sullivan led Binney into an adjoining room which was simply furnished with two odd desks and a couple of old, wooden file cabinets. The Judge helped himself to a seat, looked at his watch, and then said, "I have a rather large stamp collection. Started it in Nineteen Ten. Got bored with it in the Thirties. Roosevelt wanted to buy it from me but he never made a decent offer .... I also have a jar full of Indian Head pennies."

"You've got the wrong Sullivan!"

"Well, I'll finish my coffee and go. Where is my—"

Sullivan called off, "Ann, would you please bring the Judge's coffee in here."

When the woman returned with the cup and saucer that Binney had purposefully left in the living room, the Judge grabbed her wrist gently and said, "I'm sure I saw you around Washington in the old days. You worked for Harry Hopkins."

"Harry Hopkins? You must be kidding. How old do you think I am?"

The telephone rang. The man said lazily, "It's probably a wrong number. Nobody ever calls on that line. Answer it, will you Ann?"

The woman picked the telephone up, said "Hello?" listened for a second and then said, "I'm sorry, you have the wrong number. There's no Mr. Smith here.

The Judge suddenly started choking on his coffee. Both Sullivan and the woman rushed to his aide as the cup fell from his hand and he began to gasp for air. Sullivan undid the Judge's tie and the woman felt his pulse professionally. The Judge suddenly lurched up, agonizingly, as if he was about to take his last breath. There was a small .32 caliber revolver half hidden in his right hand. He shot the man through the breast bone and then flung him away with a pushing kick. His left hand locked over the woman's wrist and pulled her closer as he shot her in the temple. Leaping clear of the two collapsing bodies, the Judge decided that they didn't look dead enough. He shot them each once again, placed the pistol on the desk, and strode out of the house thinking how much he hated to part with the revolver.

J. Edgar Hoover had given it to him in 1936 and told him it had been taken off the body of John Dillinger. He had never taken it out of its presentation case until the previous evening when he had worn gloves to insert the new cartridges.

## 54

Braddock insisted that Ray drop out of sight and secret himself in a safe house until whatever Binney had put into motion could be neutralized. Ray chose a camp on the Texas-Louisiana border so he could get in some largemouth bass fishing while he was hiding. Braddock found him there one evening propped up on his bed with a very big pistol in a shoulder holster and half asleep. He slammed the screen door to get Ray's attention and then said, "You're one hell of a secret agent. The Seventh Army could bivouac in here without alerting you."

"I'm trying to enjoy myself. You have six guys watching me day and night."

"Not anymore my friend. You're on your own."

"What happened? Did Congress just take another slice out of your budget?"

Braddock looked around the one room cabin. Ray read his thoughts and said, "There's a pitcher of martinis in the ice box."

"When did you start drinking martinis?" Braddock made his way across the room to the refrigerator.

"They're for you. The guy at the gas station called me after you stopped in and asked for directions to this shack. I love these small, southern towns. If you're real friendly with the locals, they're your best protection. I think it's in one of our training manuals."

"It's also in the Little Red Book." Braddock took a pitcher and a glass out of the refrigerator. "I see you also chilled the glass for me. I don't get this kind of service at home."

"What's up?" asked Ray.

"Scratch Binney. As far as we can ascertain, his stroke was for real. And scratch Control. They self-destructed."

Braddock savored the drink in his hand and explained, "The police found a couple murdered in Queens. Their house was obviously some sort of command post, running the whole show. There were files, an archaic radio net. Almost all their functioning operatives were erased when you and Simon went back to war and he got the worst of it."

"When Company B went back to war!"

"We ran down a few dropouts and cripples. The only one we can't nail is the guy that did the job in Queens."

"Whoever he is, God bless him."

"We haven't got anything solid to go on yet, but it was something set up late in the war on a high level. The think tank assumes that we made a deal with certain high-ranking Nazis for God knows what. Probably atomic secrets or materials. Whatever it was, they created a team to keep the deal under wraps and watch over the krauts they spirited out of Europe."

"Now we know what happened to Borman, Mengele, and the rest of the gang."

"It's a horrible thought isn't it?"

"Were the guys at the shopping center actually krauts?"

"G.I.s! Sort of."

"Don't tell Simon about that. It'll destroy him."

"Don't be in a hurry to shed any tears. Regular G.I.s wouldn't have self-destructed so easily. This group was handpicked from former members of the German-American bund and allied organizations. They were rabid pro-Nazis."

"And they all knew?"

"In general terms. Even the bellboy. He finally made a clean breast of it."

"I guess that this gives our Crowell Collier stunt a kick in the ass?"

"Not at all. It gives us a ready-made set-up."

"Really? What does the President say about that?"

"What is he going to do about it? Deny it? Admit that this country made a deal with a bunch of top Nazis years ago and has been sheltering them ever since?"


## 55


Art Norman, Simon's son-in-law, had arranged Morris's funeral, and, along with Sam, had seen to it that it was carried out exactly as Simon dictated from his hospital bed. They buried Ankhorn in his place of birth in Pennsylvania in the most expensive casket they could find and flew in as many "B Company" and "1st Battalion" veterans as they could in the short time allotted to them.

A son from Morris's first and only marriage turned up, the marriage he never returned to after his National Guard Unit was activated on December 9th, 1941. The son, a rather dumb securities salesman from a Philadelphia suburb, and his wife, called the office almost every day inquiring about Morris's will. Art held the matter in abeyance for Simon to deal with when he returned to work.

## 56

Simon looked fantastic on his first day back at the office. He was twenty pounds lighter and, despite all, feeling better than he had in years. Open-heart surgery was ruled out and he was put on a program that included a strict diet and exercise. There was, however, a subtle change in his character. Art found himself promoted from "the son-in-law" to "my hard working partner with no crazy ideas about movies."

On that first day back, after a short, initial conference with his senior staff, Simon went through a pile of incoming correspondence dictating replies rapidly. When he came upon two letters from Germany responding to his advertisement, he put them aside with indifference and finished taking care of the rest of his mail. After he re-read the memo from Art Norman about Morris's son inquiring about an "estate," he walked down to the controller's office, went into an open safe, unlocked a smaller safe inside, and removed a metal box from it. He thumbed through a stack of thick manila envelopes until he came to one with the words "Morris Ankhorn" scrawled across it. He then called a house attorney, along with Art Norman, and his secretary Cathy, into his office to witness the opening of the envelope.

He announced, "Morris gave this to me for safekeeping ten years ago, the first time he was sick."

Simon passed the envelope to Cathy who passed it to the lawyer who opened it. The attorney glanced at a single page will which was on top of all the other papers in the envelope and said, "He made you his sole heir."

"Shit!" said Simon.

"He didn't have much to leave, did he?" said Art.

Simon's girl, Cathy, said, "His apartment. It's worth about two hundred thousand today. You gave it to him."

"What else is there?" asked Simon.

"Stock certificates," said the attorney looking at the rest of the material in the envelope.

"All junk!" said Simon. "He never invested, he gambled."

Simon's girl took the envelope from the attorney and said, "I'll take out the shares in the co-op." Pre-thinking Simon, she added, "I suppose you want to give them to his son."

Simon nodded. The girl shook her head as she went through the certificates. "Oh, well, he kept his G.I. insurance paid up, but the rest of it looks like trash. I never heard of any of these companies. She stopped speaking suddenly, removed a stock certificate from the pile, took two quick steps to the desk with it, and placed it in front of Simon with a quizzical shrug. He looked at it out of the side of his eye without any real interest. It was made out to a "Lily Kuris" and it read, "One Share of Capital Stock .... The 389 West 83rd Street Corporation."

With an affected yawn, giving nothing away, Simon smoothly said, "When Morris bought junk, he really bought junk. Look, the will is very embarrassing! I don't want to be left his dollar ninety-eight. Let's see what his other safe deposit box turns up. I have the key. Everybody back to work, except you, Cathy."

When they left the room, Simon's girl said, "He had it for years."

"Well, what can we do about it? He was always a grade "A" schmuck when it came to business. He just tried to work a jiggle on his own." He flipped the stock certificate over and looked at the back. "He even started to forge an endorsement and chickened out. Poor Morris, he tried to steal someone's building and got himself killed in the process."

Simon's Girl said, "You want the building that bad. You're the sole beneficiary of his life insurance policy."

"Is there anything else of value in there?"

"Zilch!"

"I don't think Morris wanted to leave me anything."

"His son's been calling here almost every day. He sounds like an ass... and his wife. Forget about her."

"Don't blame the son. Morris walked away from a young wife when he went overseas and never even wrote her as far as I know. Type up another will! Leave two-thirds to the son, one-third to Ray Warren, and throw in five thousand bucks apiece to each of my kids. Call up the son and tell him I'll give him the cash value of the policy and the cash equivalent of his share of the estate immediately for a release so he doesn't have to wait for probate and the apartment to be sold."

The girl coughed politely. "Who's going to sign and notarize this new will?"

Simon looked up into the air and said, "I wish Mrs. Brady was still with us. When we needed a signature in a hurry and couldn't find the body, she'd sign for them. I used to tell her, with her talent, she was in the wrong business."

Simon's girl said, "I don't think we have to go that far. He never did much work around here and since he was never around when you needed him, his secretary made him sign a stack of blank letterheads. I think they're still in his desk."

"Steve in accounting is a notary. Take care of that little matter, but first call up a travel agent.'"

"You'd better take me along in case this blows up in our faces."

"There's nothing to worry about. I'm just taking another vacation. Things are running smoothly here, right? Book me to Munich first class and reserve a car and a hotel for a week."

"May I ask, why Munich? You found the stock certificate."

"That's only one share, there may be more and there's still a lot of other things I have to straighten out in my own way. Cathy, so our stories don't get mixed up, tell Gilda, tell her I went to visit a sick, old, army buddy. She hates them. She won't ask to go along."

"An army buddy in Munich?"

"I know it sounds ridiculous, but it'll take her two weeks to figure that out and I'll be home by then."

Simon called Jane in Hollywood and wished her luck with the picture and then started to dial Ray's number. He changed his mind thinking, "Some C.I.A. agent. I'll show him how to jiggle. With all his hocus pocus, he still hasn't got the least idea what's going on. I'll show him how a businessman gets things done."

# 57

Simon stepped out of the rented red Opel and into the cold Munich air. He crossed the street to Number 38. It bore no resemblance to the structure he was looking for. He got back into the car and drove the length of Widenmeyer Street to its termination at the Maximillian Bridge and back again, several times, without finding a building that looked remotely like the one in New York. He then drove back to Number 38 and parked. He felt totally distressed.

He thought, hopefully, "They just put up a new facade." He got out of the Opel once more and returned to Number 38 and stared at the building. Totally confused, he was about to return to his car when he saw an elderly woman clad in an expensive fur coat walking a French poodle in the riverside park opposite. Simon crossed the street and went up to her. He asked, "Pardon me, do you speak English?"

"Not very well," said the woman.

"I was wondering about that building?" Simon turned and pointed to Number 38. "Has it been, a, modernized?"

The woman smiled and then said, "It wasn't thirty eight."

"No?" said Simon. "How do you know what?"

The woman smiled again. "Every once in a while someone comes to see that building you're interested in. It was on the corner by the bridge."

Simon looked off in that direction and then asked, "When did they tear it down?"

"They didn't tear it down," said the woman. "There was the big air raid. The British at night."

"You're wrong," replied Simon. "I saw that building in Nineteen Forty-five."

"No, I am not mistaken. I'll never forget that raid. It was the biggest of the war. And I remember that building well. A rich man here gave it to his mistress. Then an American's mistress heard the story and demanded that he give her a building. He gave her a copy, right?"

"Shit!" thought Simon thinking back to the first time he caught sight of 389 West 83rd Street. "She's probably right! But what made me think—"

## 58

When Simon returned to the Hilton Hotel, he asked at the desk for messages. The clerk told him, "A Doctor Strugg stopped by to see you. He waited for about an hour. He said he'd try you again tomorrow."

"Thanks," said Simon. He picked the day's newspapers to see if his second advertisement had been placed and returned to his room where he dialed Strugg's number. There was no answer. As soon as he hung up, the phone rang. Simon picked it up and said, "Hello?"

The voice on the other end of the wire said in English, "Are you the man who placed the publicity in the paper?"

"Right!" said Simon. "Who is this?"

"You're wrong to be involved with Strugg. I know. I stopped by earlier. He was waiting in the lobby of your hotel."

"Who is this?" asked Simon adamantly.

"Von Eck. That's all I can tell you now."

"You know about the building?" asked Simon.

"My father does!"

"When can I meet your father?" asked Simon.

"Why was Strugg in the hotel lobby? That wasn't a co-incidence."

"He saw the same ad you did."

"He knows nothing. He is only looking to cause trouble. He's a very dangerous man. A former S.D. officer. I can't begin to tell you how many good people he was responsible for hanging. He worked for the Allies immediately after the surrender. He should have been shot."

"I agree with you whole heartedly," said Simon with convincing enthusiasm. "If I had my way, I would have shot them all."

"Precisely!" said Von Eck." It's good to hear that. I will arrange to have you meet my father in the morning. Make sure you're not followed.

## 59

He had gray eyes and an extremely fair complexion. His face maintained an eerie, babyish charm although he was well into his seventies if not older. When Simon came down into the lobby of the Hilton and turned towards the door, Strugg rose from a leather couch and called out, "Mr. Blake?"

"Yes?" asked Simon.

Strugg reached out and shook Simon's hand stiffly. He then reached into his pocket and removed a case from which he took a calling card. It read, "Doctor Eric Strugg, Underpresident, Bavarian State Police, Retired."

Simon pocketed the card and said, "How about some breakfast?"

"Yes, I'd like breakfast. But here, it's so expensive."

"Don't worry about it," said Simon. He took Strugg by the arm and led him past the desk into the coffee shop and to a table against the window that looked out on the swimming pool. Strugg glanced at the menu and then made a face. "The prices here are ridiculous. Not too far away-"

"Don't worry about it," said Simon again. "It's on me." After they had ordered, Simon said, "Well, do you know where I can find those stock certificates?"

"Possibly," said Strugg. "One of them at least. That's why I wanted to speak with you."

"Possibly isn't good enough."

"Please, let me explain. I'm not sure we're talking about the same certificate or even if there were any involved."

"I don't get you," said Simon.

"When I was still active with the police there was a matter here in Germany that intrigued me. A missing piece of evidence. It may have been a stock certificate."

"May have been? That's it?"

"The name of the company that issued the shares was stated in your publicity as the Three Eighty Nine West Eighty-third Street Corporation, correct?"

"Yes," said Simon.

"That had to do with the ownership of a residential building in New York City?"

"Right," said Simon.

"In this old case, there was talk of the ownership of a residential building in New York City. Do you mind if I take notes? My memory doesn't work for me so well anymore."

"No, go ahead."

"Thank you. If you don't mind, I would like to know your interest in this stock certificate?"

"I came to Munich to ask questions, not answer them!" said Simon.

"Please, if we can clarify some details, I may be able to help answer them for you. We can help each other."

Simon was silent for a moment. He then said, "Okay, I sized you up. I think I can trust you." He told Strugg the whole story. When he finished, Strugg said, "Judge Binney. I didn't know he was still alive. I met him once, briefly, a long time ago. Yes, he could very well be involved in an attack on your person now that you explained everything to me."

"How does it all tie into the building in New York?"

"I don't know yet. I think I can resolve that matter for you shortly. Let me ask, you were an officer during the war? Panzer? I don't know the English word."

"Tanks!" said Simon. "I was a Sergeant! How did you know?"

This time Strugg smiled. "Mr. Blake, I came here on a simple matter. Murder! I think that you've handed me something much more important. You know, it always happens like that. You arrest a prostitute and she turns in her pimp. You arrest the pimp and he turns in a burglar. You arrest a burglar in he turns in a murderer. You catch the murderer and—"

"And what?"

"I think I may be able to find your missing certificates. One at least. I'll need a day."

"A day! Great! That sounds like good old German efficiency. Bill me anything reasonable. Double reasonable."

Strugg pushed his chair back and got to his feet. "Thank you for breakfast." As he walked away from the table Simon called after him, "Mr. Strugg!"

"Yes?" replied the old man.

"What did you do in the war?" asked Simon sarcastically.

"The same thing I'm doing now. A cop!"

## 60

Von Eck, a thin, studious, young man met Simon outside a sex shop on the Marienplatz and then led him into City Hall, and up three flights of stairs to a coffee shop crowded with housewives taking a break from their weekly shopping. He took him to a room in the rear and up to an elderly, heavy set, gray haired woman seated alone at a table against the wall.

As Simon drew nearer, he said to Von Eck, "I thought we were going to meet your father?"

Von Eck pulled out a chair for Simon, sat in his own chair, and whispered, "This is my father."

The buxom woman nodded politely as Simon glanced around nervously wondering what exactly he had gotten himself into. After ordering three beers, she said in German, "Is he still alive?"

"Binney?" asked Simon in return.

"Not the colonel. The man. Tell me, is he still alive?"

Simon wet his lips and asked, "The man?"

"The owner of the building?" whispered Von Eck.

"Crowell Collier?" asked Simon.

"Who?" asked the woman with great irritation.

"Max Geisler?" asked Simon with almost too much playfulness for the situation.

"You're insulting me!" said the woman.

"Rolph Liebhomm."

"All trash! You're insulting me." The woman turned to Von Eck. "This man's an impostor. He didn't come from Binney. You've endangered me."

Von Eck replied rapidly, "No father! He's only testing you." He asked Simon in English, "You're only testing him, aren't you?"

The woman motioned Simon closer and whispered into his ear, "Max Geisler was the impersonator. Rolph Liebhomm was the commander of the guest house. Commander? A joke. He died there."

"No!" said Simon. To Von Eck he said, "I don't think you guys are on the up and up."

Von Eck shot out of his chair. "Please! Mr. Blake, we are reliable!" He turned to the woman and said, "Father?"

The woman took Simon by the hand and said, "Come!" She led him into an alcove, past the rest rooms, and through a modern fire door. Von Eck handed the waitress some money to pay for their beers and hurried after them.

They climbed an old, stone stair until they came to a heavy wooden door. The woman opened it, waved Simon and Von Eck inside, and said, "We'll have privacy here."

Von Eck shut the door. When Simon's eyes adjusted to the darkness he found himself looking at the mechanism of the Glockenspiel. A circle of Bavarian knights, ladies in waiting, courtiers, pages, heralds, and coopers, waited patiently to begin their daily pageant.

The woman put her shopping bag down in front of one of the huge, vertical gears that meshed with the turntables and switched on an overhead light. She stood erect and said, "You don't trust me because you don't know who I am." Then she unpinned her wig and lifted it off of her head carefully to reveal a bald head. Simon felt himself about to break into laughter.

The woman stepped forward, grabbed the overhead lamp, and directed it at her own face, which looked very much like a man's. "Now, tell me, is he still alive?"

"I really don't have the slightest idea who you are," said Simon.

"I'm the man you came to see. General Heinrich Müller! I was commanding officer of the Gestapo! Now, tell me, is he still alive?"

"Who, Geisler?" Simon broke out into laughter. Von Eck and the old man joined him. Suddenly, Simon said in German, "I can't believe this. I came up here expecting a bunch of anti-Nazi vigilantes and I found a war criminal. You are so ludicrous, I can't even hate you anymore! I mean, really, is that the way you eluded everyone all these years? Pretending to be your own widow? Tell me, Müller, are you wearing panty hose under that outfit or are you still old fashioned? I love this. I mean, how could a whole nation like Germany put a bunch of addled brain guys like you in charge?"

Müller suddenly stopped laughing and screamed, "You're talking Jewish not German. A Jew! The Führer would not send a Jew. This is a trap!" Müller slapped Von Eck to stop him laughing. "You idiot! After all these years, your stupidity finally betrayed me. Kill him."

"With what?" muttered Von Eck nervously.

"With your bare hands. He's only a Jew!"

Von Eck spotted a coil of wire on a work table, said, "I'll hang him." and approached Simon. "I'll tie your hands first."

Simon said, "Not this Jew you don't!" He punched Von Eck in the jaw, knocking him clear over the work table and then cracked him over the head with a heavy wrench. As Von Eck slid to the floor, Simon looped the coil of wire around his neck. "Now let's see how you like hanging."

Müller reached for his shopping bag and started to throw out the groceries inside as Von Eck came back to his senses and felt the wire around his throat. He began to scream. Simon dropped hold of the wire and started towards Müller. He demanded, "What have you got in that bag, old lady?"

Müller reached into his shopping bag and freed a small, Beretta pistol that was entangled in some knitting, cocked it, and raised it to fire as Simon knocked him sprawling against the works of the glockenspiel. Müller got one shot off, missing Simon completely.

Simon slapped the Beretta out of Müller's hand and said, "Put on your wig." I'm going to take you back to the States dressed like that and display you in a store front on Fifth Avenue."

Müller scrambled backwards up a steep flight of stairs and onto the upper turntable of the glockenspiel.

Simon climbed up after him cautiously.

Müller stood, glaring at Simon with defiance, his eyes shifting about, searching for an escape route. Just then, the hour was struck and the turntable started to revolve. The crowd on the Marienplatz below gasped in unison as Müller appeared in the tower above. Simon stepped out into their line of sight and reached for Müller who leaped to the outer turntable only to find himself being carried forward towards Simon.

As Simon reached for Müller's arm, his jacket caught on the bridle of the mounted knight coming up behind him, giving Müller time to strike out with both fists. Simon stumbled back onto the rim of the outer turntable, lost his footing, and dragged forward by the knight, slipped off the outer edge of the niche, to dangle by his ensnared jacket and one free hand over the Marienplatz below.

Müller, quick stepping to stay in place, looked down at Simon and said, "To kill one more Jew will make it all worthwhile."

The lance of the Bavarian knight on the inner turntable swung outward to its left and aimed for the breast plate of its opponent from whose stirrup Simon was being dragged. As Müller started to stomp down on Simon's left hand and send him hurtling into the crowd below, the point of the lance caught him between his shoulder blades and lifted him up onto the knight on the other side of the lift, crushing his neck, and grinding inwards until the mechanism of the glockenspiel locked, the gears stripped, and the clock ground to a halt.

Simon did not see any of this as he struggled to maintain his grasp with his left hand and find a handhold for his right in the freezing, slick, stone facade. He suddenly felt five strong fingers close around his right wrist and found himself being pulled up to safety. Another strong, young hand secured his left arm and he was swung back onto the turntable like a young child.

"For God sakes, thanks!" gasped Simon to the young men in blue ski parkas who helped him off the turntable and back down into the work shop. "I want to take care of both of you. I'll make you rich."

"It's only our duty," said one of the young men. "State Police."

They had Von Eck on the landing below in handcuffs. As Simon was led down to the ground floor of the tower, Strugg looked up at him with a soft smile and said, "Please, you'll have to excuse me. But I'm not much good at running upstairs anymore."

"I suppose I have you to thank," said Simon as a paramedic attended to his lacerated hands.

"Only in a way," said Strugg.

"You had me followed, right?" said Simon.

"True! It took a little time. I'm retired and they don't listen to me that readily anymore at headquarters. Luckily, the concierge at your hotel knew your destination. We didn't expect to find you hanging from the Glockenspiel. Quite interesting! When I spoke to you this morning, I thought you were a bit insane. I had no idea there were any old Nazis involved, especially Müller. He was second on my list."

"Then why did you have me followed?" asked Simon.

"The first on my list. Another war criminal!" replied Strugg.

"I don't understand?"

"I was curious to see what you were doing in Germany again. The stock certificate you are looking for? There is another? One that you've had it in your possession since you murdered the woman."

"What woman?" asked Simon. "You're starting to talk gibberish like those other two guys."

"A very strange case. She was born in the United States, brought back here with her parents, and then returned after the first war. For some reason she was naturalized in Nineteen Twenty Four with the help of your friend, Judge Binney. She was what you called a showgirl. A mistress of Crowell Collier. She made powerful friends here in the Thirties. This Collier, he made her many gifts including an interest in that building."

"Okay," said Simon. "That's the woman I'm looking for. What's this bull about murder?"

"I'm not finished. This woman. She was an American citizen twice over and I think an agent of the OSS I have the feeling that you were in Steinhoffen towards the very end of the war and that you murdered her for the money and jewels she received from Binney. You used the same money to buy real estate once you left the army. One million dollars or more. Why the stock certificate? Why did you take that? That's the only concrete evidence of your crime."

"You're out of your mind, Strugg!" said Simon. "Are you accusing me of stealing a million dollars during the war?"

"And murder!"

"You're nuts on both counts! How would I get back to the States lugging a million bucks?"

"That's why I assumed you were a Panzer officer. A panzer would be a convenient place to hide such a large sum. I also think that there were others involved. Officers! Maybe only one officer with a business background who stayed in Europe after the war and arranged to transfer the funds, say, through Switzerland."

"Strugg!" said Simon incensed. "Don't try to pin that one on me. I was in Steinhoffen less than ten hours and I didn't see any woman with a million dollars. You can ask anyone in my outfit."

"That's what I intend to do," said Strugg.

## 61

Ray Warren waited anxiously outside the customs area in the British Airways terminal for the passengers aboard the Concord from London to appear. When Simon approached, Ray's mouth dropped. His friend finally looked old, real old, and there was much more gray in his hair than he had ever seen before. Ray rushed forward to embrace him. "You crazy idiot, you could have gotten yourself killed nailing Müller."

"How did you know about that?" asked Simon in a daze. "They were supposed to keep it quiet."

"The grapevine."

Simon just stared ahead as if Ray wasn't present and said, "They got us by the balls, Ray. I walked right into it with that Goddamn building. We didn't see that building in Munich, we saw a *picture* of the house in Steinhoffen we requisitioned as a billet."

"What?"

Simon took Ray out of earshot of the porter carrying his luggage and said, "A Goddamn kraut detective put it all together. Steinhoffen! Morris had one of the stock certificates all along. He took it from the house we looted."

"So what?" said Ray. "It doesn't mean beans. It was too long ago. Nobody can prove anything. The whole outfit would stand up for us."

"I'm not so sure they will, Ray. Morris murdered the old lady! He kicked the shit out of her and tried to force her to endorse the certificate over to him."

"Come on? Morris?" Ray digested Simon's words and then their full import hit him. A stunned look appeared on his face. "When?"

"We left her alone with him. Remember, after we grabbed the loot and took our baths. One of the other tank crews invited us over to their house where they had booze and young broads."

"I thought he was only going to fuck her. He liked them with experience."

"Bastard!" said Simon. "After we left he went through the rest of the stuff and found the stock certificate. He tortured her to death... Ray!"

"I still can't believe Morris did that, but if he did I would have stood up for him. Don't forget, she was the enemy!"

"She was an American! She was an OSS operative, Ray! She tried to tell us back then, but we didn't pay attention to her."

"OSS?"

"Where the hell do you think she got all those greenbacks?"

Ray nodded and then shook his head sadly. "Now I see. She welcomed us with open arms like she expected us. She got the satchel out from under the bed and said to you, 'Here, take care of the money.' She had a mink coat on and was dressed to kill. She wasn't waiting for a conquering army, she was waiting for friends. She was one of us." Ray shook his head again. "That explains it. That explains it all. She was part of Binney's group! God damn it, there was that OSS tag team waiting outside of town for us to secure Steinhoffen. The young idiot Lieutenant who couldn't believe it was under fire. They were there to bring her in, but we found her first. They should have said something. She should have tried to explain herself."

"Morris told her to shut up or he'd shoot her," said Simon.

Ray shrugged. "We owe Binney an apology. I'm willing to bet he knew we were responsible for killing one of his agents and that he probably hushed it up all these years. I mean, no wonder he tried to have us killed. Turning up and threatening to expose him when we had something more dreadful to hide."

"Yes," said Simon dully. "We owe him an apology."

"I'll take care of it, but get it out of your system. It was Morris's fault. It was the war."

"But I was the only one that really profited from it," said Simon.

"Don't feel guilty because your buddies blew their shares on wine, woman, and song."

## 62

Binney's girl showed Simon and Ray into the Judge's office and they declined her offer of coffee. She brought in a large carafe anyway in case they changed their minds. The Judge appeared a few moments later in a wheelchair pushed by Parri. Expending a great effort, Binney managed to instruct Parri to leave the room. When the young man was gone, he leaped to his feet, rushed to the door, and locked it. With Simon and Ray looking on in amazement, the Judge went to the sideboard, poured himself a steaming cup of coffee, and said, "I used to wonder why a handsome, athletic, young man such as Parri wastes his time taking care of an old man like me. I finally realized that it's because he's stupid. Of course, I judge everyone by my own standards and there are few men in the world as smart as yours truly. I'm sorry that he took so long in warning you about Control. I shouldn't have felt sorry for giving the orders to have you killed, but I did. Fortunately, you both helped resolve the matter to everyone's satisfaction."

Simon got up and placed the stock certificate on Binney's desk.

The Judge barely glanced at it. "How did you know she was carrying all that money?"

"She just handed it to us. We picked her house only because it had a decent bathtub," said Simon.

"Bathtub!" cackled the Judge. "I never heard anything so funny in my life and I'm eighty six years old, give or take a day. Lily was too smart for her own good. The code word was White Wash. She never got it right. Well, no harm done."

"No harm done?" said Simon. "Morris murdered her!"

"Does that really disturb you?" asked the Judge.

"Are you kidding?" said Simon.

"How long have you know Ankhorn?" the Judge challenged.

"Since Forty One."

"And you believe he was the type of person to kill an unarmed woman?" asked the Judge. "Come on!"

"How did he get the stock certificate?"

"She gave it to him. He promised to talk you two into giving the money back in exchange. He was quite taken by Lily."

"How do you know?"

"She told me. You see, your outfit was nowhere near Stienhoffen when she was killed. You were long gone. It's all in the records. I caught up with her later. Of course, you're not entirely blameless. There was a matter of some coded signals she was supposed to turn over to the OSS She refused to do it until the money you took was replaced. I wasn't bound to dig up another million dollars for her, so I just worked her over a bit until I got the information we needed. Being in the legal game all my life, I knew the folly of leaving a witness to Operation White Wash, so she had to go. Of course, officially, I've never been to Steinhoffen. Strugg's a plugger though. He may zero in on the money. Tell him you won it on the ship going home. Knowing him, he'll take ten years to check out the other troops on board and he doesn't have ten years left. Case dismissed." The Judge removed three new stock certificates from a folder on his desk and handed them to Simon. "Next matter! After I confirmed your identities back then, I studied the matter and entered a Spoils of War Decision. You won't find it quoted anyplace, so don't bother looking. I directed the Three Eighty Nine West Eighty-third Street Corporation to increase its shares outstanding to six and issued one to each of you. I've been paying out all the net income to another Max Geisler, and, I repeat another Max Geisler, the owner of record of the other three shares. It wasn't quite legal, but I don't think you're in a position to challenge me publicly on that point. Mr. Geisler will let those three shares go at an equitable price."

"I don't want the building anymore," said Simon.

"You have no choice in the matter. You came to a party to which you weren't invited and you won the door prize. I'm retiring. Operation White Wash is yours."

Ray said, "I don't get you. This guy with the other three shares?"

"Not a war criminal if that's what you think. I would not have, in any way, shape, or form, let one of those bastards off the hook. He's just a poor, old man. And when I call them old, they are old! Parri will arrange an appointment with him so you can clear your minds." A touch of fatigue crept into the Judge's voice. "Blake, I'll work something out with the Armanda Collier foundation as per the rest of the block front. I drew up the original stipulation, I'm in the best position to challenge it."

# 63

After they left his office, the Judge thought, Those two think they're real smart, but they're not. They bought the story about my killing Lily in the line of duty without question. It wasn't exactly that way. For some strange reason she acted decently. She turned over the signals voluntarily. Of course, she bitched about the money. I would have never known where to find her if she didn't. They sent me to Steinhoffen to try to calm her down and make other arrangements in her interest. She never expected that. I guess she thought they flew me back to the States with the others.

The reason for my killing Lily was the only lie, the only lie in the whole story. Of course, thought the Judge, Blake and Warren left here assuming that I had lied about not making any deals with Nazis. I wonder what their reaction would have been if I had told them "White Wash" was set up to protect one man and one man alone, Adolph Hitler.

Of course I didn't let it happen. I was too smart for that. I told Rolph in the privacy of my room at the guest house, "The reason that your defensive positions are so poor and they refuse to let you improve them is because they're setting this place up for a commando-like raid and they want it to go as smoothly as possible. The Waffen SS will leave at their regular time and there will be nothing left here but a group of tired, untrained, middle-aged men in fancy *uniforms*."

"They wouldn't do that to us!" replied Rolph.

"They already have. Every man in your outfit will be dead by dawn... They're not going to leave any witnesses."

"Including me?" asked Rolph.

"Especially you," I replied. "Rolph, if you want to be alive when the sun comes up in the morning, you only have to do one simple thing for me.

"What?" asked Rolph with suspicion.

"What you see with the room numbers changed is the military mind trying to make things neat and simple. Rearrange the numbers on the doors of the rooms as they should be. The odds and evens on opposite sides of the hall."

"How is that going to help?"

"If I'm right, the assault party will kill the man in room Two. If you don't do as I say, that man will be Max Geisler. Who would you prefer that they killed if I'm correct? Your beloved Führer or Max?"

Rolph didn't hesitate answering. "The bastard next door in Three!"

"If I'm wrong and there is no raid tonight, you just shift the numbers back before dawn and no one will be wiser."

"In any case, it's the end for me, yes?" asked Rolph.

"No!" I replied. "Do you have civilian clothes with you?"

"Yes! It's generally agreed among the men here that we put them on and flee at the first sight of the American army.

"After the Waffen SS leave, you come up here and get out of your uniform. Bring some shoe polish for your hair."

"For my hair?"

"You're going to impersonate Max Geisler. I think I can convince them that having another live Max Geisler is a good thing."

"What about Max?"

"He's going to become the bastard next door. He's good at it isn't he? I think people will be watching. Watching to see if we keep our word."

After Rolph left, I went to Max's room. He listened to my plan and then nodded in agreement. Later, when the boys from the Waffen SS left the guest house for the night, Rolph relieved the floor guard and we changed the numbers on all of the rooms. He then put on a set of civilian clothes and we shared a bottle of brandy as we waited.

The raid took place that night as I had expected. My reasoning was simple. The bastard in Room Three couldn't be out of sight of his own subordinates for more than twenty-four hours at a time.

When I heard the plane at three a.m. sharp and the first distant mortar explosion at exactly three twenty, I congratulated myself.

Volunteers from my own airborne battalion firing from the ridge I had identified earlier destroyed the sandbagged emplacements in less than five seconds as other men of my unit attacked the annex, filled with sleeping, honorary SS, with white phosphorous grenades. The few that made it out of the windows and doors were shot down at close range. Co-currently, two squads of OSS men infiltrated the lower floors of the guest house killing a cook and someone staying up late writing in the dining room. The other squad reached the second floor through the window of one of the unoccupied rooms and shot the guard in the room facing the stairs.

They then shot the lock off of the door of my room. I stood in front of Rolph with my hands in the air and shouted, "I'm Colonel Binney. The man in Room Three goes with us."

"We know!" replied one of them. He then said, "Let's hit the road, Colonel."

"He comes, too," I said pointing at Rolph.

"There's only supposed to be two of you."

"He goes or I stay!"

As we went out the door, two other OSS men were escorting Geisler down the hall towards us. They had placed a hood over his head so that he wouldn't be recognized. As I turned to race down the stairs, I caught sight of an olive drab garbed figure armed with a flame thrower. He didn't even bother to open the door of the cell. He thrust the nozzle of the weapon through the peephole, pressed the trigger, and filled the interior with a burst of blazing napalm. I didn't even hear a scream.

We double timed all the way back to the main highway where a solitary, camouflaged C-47 with engines running awaited us. An Air Corps Master Sergeant gave me some flap about the extra passenger, but I overruled him. We landed at a blacked out, secret airfield in France. Geisler, still hooded, was immediately transferred to another plane.

When Donavan learned what I had done, he shouted, "You destroyed the whole purpose of the mission."

I replied, "No I didn't! We have a pretty good Hitler to parade around and we didn't kill Max Geisler. He's standing here right next to me. And, we left a body for the Russians to find. I don't make any deals with criminals."

"If you didn't have the friends you do, they'd be finding your body in the rubble."

## 64

The Judge made a point to introduce Simon and Ray to the old man who owned the three other shares in the building.

After they left his Park Avenue apartment, Ray asked, "Who do you think the old guy really is?"

"Some guy named Kuris'," replied Simon. "Leave me alone already!"

"Come on. Think!"

"Max Geisler," said Simon, "but put a big maybe in front. Who do you think he is?"

"Crowell Collier!" said Ray. "There's no doubt about it. I know I can't prove it, but I have, this feeling. He's at least ninety. Geisler was younger."

"He was in pretty good shape for ninety," said Simon.

Simon bought the three shares of the 389 West 83rd Street Corporation held by the old man and the two held by Morris's estate and Ray Warren. Without much enthusiasm he started negotiations with the Armanda Collier Foundation for the rest of the block front. The tenants living in the brownstones organized and fiercely defended the stipulation in Armanda's will protecting Three Eighty Nine from demolition and tried to get it declared a landmark.

A young architect, Jim Coleman, stood outside of the building with Simon and said. "It's not a landmark and not very distinguished. Steel beams and masonry supporting walls. It's not a reproduction of anything. It's just a typical, West side building trimmed in a mock, German Renaissance style."

"I'm offering them a fortune to relocate. I don't know why they're fighting me."

"Tenants!" sighed Coleman. "Landmark? Outside of being ugly, there's one thing interesting about this building. It's contiguous with the brownstones. The floor heights are the same. I measured them before I started poking around."

"Poking around?" asked Simon.

"The second floors of all the brownstones between the building and Armanda Collier's old townhouse are all missing a total of 532 square feet of interior space. There has to be a passage way between the two."

That afternoon Simon entered the second floor apartment and began to strip the plaster from the wall of the bedroom whose interior wall abutted the first brownstone next to 389. It took him two hours. He then started ripping off the wood paneling underneath until he found a section of it that once served as a hidden door. Using the crowbar for leverage, he forced the door open and found a narrow passage blocked by bricks and mortar.

When dawn finally showed itself through the windows, he had removed enough brick to enter the passageway with a floor lamp that he had rigged up with a long extension cord. His calculations told him that it led to what would have been Crowell's bedroom in the Collier townhouse. "God damn it," he said, "That's all? Crowell used to come this way for a little fun and games after his mother hit the sack?"

Simon measured the width of the passageway. He multiplied it by the length and got exactly 420 square feet. Checking his notes, he found that the brownstone, exactly midway between the Collier townhouse and the building he owned, was missing 112 feet of floor space more than the others. He began to chip into the plaster at the center line with the crowbar. By ten am, he found another bricked-in door, but he was too tired to proceed any further.

## 65

"I want to show you something!" he said the following day as he led Ray to the hidden corridor.

"Okay!" said Warren. "Crowell had a little action going for him in the apartment building, and he didn't like to use the front door. He was afraid of momma catching him."

Simon showed Ray to the second, bricked in entrance, and said, "Give me a hand with this. The first brick is always the hardest."

"I'll do it! You just rest. Don't take any more chances with your heart."

It took Ray four hours to clear the second doorway.

When he was done, Simon added still another extension cord onto the floor lamp and poked it into the small room that they had uncovered. He said, "This is what Binney was worried about all these years! Why he drew up the will that way! Why he didn't want to sell the building until he knew that he could trust us!"

Ray looked into the cubicle over Simon's shoulder and laughed. "It's just a wine cellar. The racks are still loaded. There must be at least fifty thousand dollars' worth of booze in here. I wonder if any of the stuff is still good?" Ray removed a champagne bottle from one of the racks and blew the dust off of the label. "Nineteen Twenty One. Let's try this with dinner tonight."

"There has to be more," said Simon staring at the cases of hard liquor stacked up against the wall.

"Simon, Crowell built this tunnel to his girlfriend's apartment and put in some booze. What else does a guy want out of life?"

"There has to be more," said Simon.

"If there is, we'd better find it." He pulled the lamp into the center of the room and placed it on its side so that its light would reach into the far corners of the cubicle. His gaze swept the room and settled on a stack of liquor cases against the far wall. He said, "Give me a hand."

They only had to move two cases of scotch before they found the mummified, skeletal remains wedged against the outside wall.

Ray said, "I was wrong about the guy on Park Avenue. We just found Crowell Collier. Get another extension cord. He was murdered! There's something wrapped around his neck."

"Who did it? Binney?" asked Simon.

"Who else, but? We owe him a favor don't we?" He meant for stealing the OSS money, something they'd be forced to own up to if the Judge was displeased. "I know exactly how to take care of this."

## 66

Parri said, "There's an article about the building in the *Times* today. Shall I read it to you?"

The Judge, sitting in his wheelchair in the little garden at the rear of his cottage, nodded. Parri sat down next to him and read loudly, "Workmen demolishing a building on West Eighty-third Street broke through an interior wall yesterday to discover a secret passageway, that upon investigation, was found to lead from the former Armanda

Collier mansion in the middle of the block to the bedroom of a second floor apartment in a building on the corner of Riverside Drive. Further investigation disclosed a hidden room off this passageway that, according to one of the workman at the site, was equipped with antiquated code machines, weapons, and classified intelligence material dating back to World War One. The room was immediately sealed by court order until its contents could be examined by agents of the F.B.I. Captain Crowell C. Collier, the only son of Armanda Collier, the self-made multi-millionaire known as Lady Midas, walked out of the Collier mansion on West Eighty-Third Street on November Twenty-sixth, Nineteen Twenty Five and was never heard from since. A recently completed major Hollywood film, and a book based upon it, allude that Captain Collier, who served in the A.E.F. during World War One, had been a member of a secret United States Espionage Agency that preceded the OSS and the C.I.A. The Collier mansion is situated on the north side of West Eighty-Third Street between West End Avenue and Riverside Drive. The entire block front was assembled by the late Simon Blake, a prominent New York investor-developer who had planned-"

As Parri continued to read, the Judge thought, The boys finally took care of that matter for me. They even got that fellow Braddock involved with some ridiculousness. Of course, at first, they thought I killed Crowell. Then the autopsy proved different. Showed that he hanged himself. They may wonder why I was so embarrassed about that, but there's no way for them to find out that he was bricked up in there alive, way before the war. They'll never know that Crowell and Lily planned to run off to Germany to marry. Never know how much of a tyrant Armanda was. That she found out about the corridor and ordered me to have a couple of masons wall up the entrance in Crowell's bedroom in order to confront him in Lily's apartment. She gave Lily an hour to get out of the country and then ordered the masons to brick up the wall in that bedroom.

Lily didn't protest. She even took the money Armanda threw at her. She didn't tell us that Crowell had panicked when he heard his mother at the door and hid in the secret corridor. The note he left said that he had drunk a full bottle of scotch as he waited in the wine cellar for Armanda to go away. He couldn't imagine Lily letting both ends of the corridor be bricked up.

I didn't know. I thought that Crowell had gone ahead to the Cunard pier. I arranged the whole thing of course. He wasn't too sharp when it came to anything practical like steamship tickets. I was the one who showed him how to squeeze enough funds out of his mother's enterprises to put up the building and get out from under Armanda's thumb once and for all. I even created a new identity for him. I felt guilty. She treated me more like a son than she did him. She always expected a lot more out of Crowell. She wanted him to be some sort of martyr.

She ordered me to escort Lily to the pier. But when we got to the pier, Lily insisted I'd better not board the ship. Crowell, she claimed, was going to remain hidden in his cabin for the entire voyage.

What happened didn't dawn on me for an entire month. Even when Armanda claimed that she heard Crowell calling out to her in the early hours: That he needed help. That the Communists had swallowed him up and she would never ever see him again. I tried to convince her that it was all nonsense, but she started sleeping in his bedroom and continued to claim that she heard his voice every night. I cabled Crowell in Europe asking him to return, but received no reply. By then, Armanda, usually as sharp as a razor and as strong as a horse, was reduced to a disorientated old woman. She called me into his bedroom and said, "I'm closing up the house, Foster. I think we bricked him up in there."

I still didn't believe such a thing could be possible until one of her friends told me that Armanda didn't find the entrance to the passage by accident. That Lily had told her about it and demanded money to give up marrying her son. It was only then that I realized that Lily had planned the whole thing to rid herself of Crowell and get her hands on all the cash he had put aside at the same time.

I sent Armanda and the servants back to Ambrose that very afternoon. As soon as I loosened the first brick in the bedroom, the odor of death hit me. I had to cover my face with a handkerchief soaked in cologne just to continue on. I found him hanging from an overhead light fixture. Crowell? A decomposed, fetid, unrecognizable thing. I cut him down and laid him out as decently as I could behind the crates.

The note he left told me the rest. He had tried for days to scratch his way out with broken bottles before he decided to kill himself. He cursed his mother and me, but made no mention of Lily. I vowed then and there to kill her, but she was always too smart for me. If the war didn't come along I would have never found her. She knew I was serious about that and was all too happy to turn me in to the Gestapo. And, sometimes, I wonder if she didn't outsmart me a second time.

One day, a long time ago, the horrible thought came to me that the man I met in her apartment on Zeppelin Street may not have been Max at all. It may have actually been

Hitler. Maybe somebody figured out what my exact reactions to the situation would be and carefully programmed me to do exactly what I did. The room numbers had been switched before and Donavan wasn't nearly as upset as he should have been. There had to be a reason for that!

Of course there was the other bunker in Berlin they used later. But in all these years I never heard the Max Geisler on Park Avenue—the one who was supposed to be a comedian—say anything even remotely humorous. Could it have been Max Geisler Number One who was cremated in Room Three? Could Rolph have been a much better actor than I thought? The reality that Adolph Hitler lived to a ripe, old age in comfort as an American citizen with my support, friendship, and subsistence? And, just before I killed Lily, I seem to remember that she moaned, "I begged them not to send you. I knew this would happen to me."

If she didn't send for me, who did?

## EPILOGUE

Ray was rather fond of London and lived in a small flat on Westbourne Terrace in Bayswater. He had found a job with a multi-national company and had lost all interest in intelligence work. There was nothing he could ever do in that field to top the Crowell Collier stunt. The impact of it was enormous. He was therefore surprised when he entered the Railway Pub for a drink after work. Shocked was more like it, because the white haired old man sitting at the end of the bar was Braddock. He had aged drastically since Ray had last seen him.

Ray took a place next to Braddock and ordered a glass of wine. He said, "Has the shit hit the fan again?"

"No," said Braddock. "But I have to put you in harness again."

"Forget about it. I'm in London to stay."

"You can stay." Braddock paused and then said, "You're not going to like what I'm going to ask you to do, but you have to do it. You may, by the way, become wealthy in the process."

"Shoot." said Ray.

"You'll have to dump on that girl, Jane Scott."

"I don't read you."

"I want you to write a book—"

"I don't—"

"Someone will write it for you. I want you to write a book exposing me, the agency, and admitting the whole Crowell Collier espionage ring was just a figment of our imagination."

"I understand now," said Ray. "We did all the damage we could when the Reds took the bait, hook, line, and sinker. Now we're going to embarrass them for being that stupid. I love the idea. But Jane? Why her? This will make her look like an idiot."

"You have to take a casualty once in a while."

Ray thought about it. "Another way to run it, we can lay off the girl for a bit. Let's go ahead with the idea we had of taking Crowell's remains and exchanging them with someone in the Kremlin wall about his age. Then it'll really be paranoia time in Moscow. Then we can wait and then dump on the movie, but only if we have to."

"We can't do it that way," said Braddock.

"Why?" asked Ray.

"The body in the wine cellar wasn't Crowell's."